'An innovative, impressive and well crafted narrative that strikes a chord for young and old alike.'
Carol Leeming FRSA

PETE KALU is a storyteller and author. He has published five novels for adults and has won prizes for both his theatre plays and his poetry, including the BBC's Dangerous Comedy Award 2003. He is a PhD Creative Writing student at Lancaster University. He lives in Manchester.

BEING ME

ADELE VIALLI

Pete Kalu

hoperoad hr
publishing

HopeRoad Publishing Ltd
P O Box 55544
Exhibition Road
London SW7 2DB

www.hoperoadpublishing.com

First Published by HopeRoad 2015

A CIP catalogue for this book is available from the British Library

ISBN 978-1-908446-35-0
eISBN 978-1-908446-41-1

Printed and bound by Lightning Source

For Gina

INTRODUCTION

(which you can skip if you like)

Hi, I'm Adele Vialli and this story is made up from my diary when I was fourteen. Sometimes, the words are taken straight out of my diary, but mostly I've made the notes into chapters. I know the story is jumpy and nobody is going to accuse me of being Jacqueline Wilson or Hunger Games in disguise. Too bad. I also know that it begins with three – you will probably think boring – essays I wrote and it doesn't have everything tied up neatly at the end. I'm sorry about that, too. Unfortunately, the way this stuff happened, there was no neat and happy ending. Anyway, I hate long introductions so this one ends now. Here come the essays. You can skip them if you want (turn to page 7 to miss them out) or copy them and use them for your own school work – I won't charge you extra if you do that. Ha ha.

Oh, and you should check out my web page –
www.hoperoadpublishing.com/adele-vialli
and follow me on Twitter – @adelevialli

ESSAY ONE

Colours.

What do we mean when we say people are different? What do we mean when we say people are the same? Every Egyptian Pharaoh was different and yet every Egyptian Pharaoh we imagine to be the same. But that's all boring History. Let's talk about my favourite subject. Me. There are many things that are the same about me and you. Maybe you like bananas like I do, maybe you hate them. Maybe you have two wobbly back teeth like I do, maybe you have an annoying brother like I do. What is more unlikely is that we share any of the next stuff. I look white but I have an (half) Ethiopian grandmother so actually I am black. This leads to the question what is black? Who decides who is black and who is not? My friend Mikaela has two black parents and is dark skinned, has a big African booty, lightly curled Afro hair and can bogle. Does this make her more black than me? My dad says he is all white – as pure as the driven snow, even though, as mentioned above, his mum is half black, something his sister confirmed to me when she visited one time. And my mum is white English, from Liverpool. Also we are very rich and less black people are rich than white (though Mikaela is rich because her mum

1

and dad are both lawyers and they have a Bentley car). So if black is a scale of 1 to 10, how many do I score? We all come from Africa originally so everybody scores at least one. We are all related to the Egyptian Pharaohs. End of Essay.

Teacher's Comments:

5 out of 10.
A good try. Adele that is spoilt by your sloppy use of punctuation, the absence of any paragraphs and needless repetition. Also, think about using the third person ('he' and 'she') rather than writing essays which focus on yourself.

ESSAY TWO

Happy Families. Discuss.

Everyone wishes their family was like the card game, Happy Families, where every family is complete and complimentary. In my opinion there are two problems with 'Happy Families' and these problems are the word 'Happy' and the word, 'Families'. If I have something that can be described as a family, it is not 'happy'.

Mum.
Mum probably has a Diploma in being Miserable. She could out-misery even the entire cast of *Les Miserables*.

Arguments for and against Misery.
Let's skip this bit, it's boring.

Dad.
My dad is not worthy of the name, Dad. His sperm produced me according to Biology, but apart from driving me to school, sighing at my school reports and banging on the bathroom door to hurry me up, he makes no contribution to my life. That is because he devotes all his time to My Talented Brother (Note for teacher: more arguments for

and against my dad will be added here later).

My Talented Brother.

MTB's birth certificate name is Anthony. He is spoilt rotten by my dad and adored by my mum because (a) he is a boy and (b) because he has won trophies in football. The fact that I myself have won trophies in football slips Dad's mind. Many other things slip Dad's mind where MTB is concerned. Like fairness. Chores. And giving me the same amount of pocket money as MTB had at my age. Animal Farm by George Orwell got it right. Although all people are equal, some, like MTB, are more equal than others. This is an injustice. End of Essay.

Teacher's Comments:

5 out of 10.

Another good try, Adele and well done on the lovely paragraphs. Perhaps you should think about planning your essay before you write it? Also, you cannot simply say 'I will finish this bit later' within an essay, you need to actually finish it.

ESSAY THREE

Ghosts.

Definition: People who die but come back from the dead to haunt others.

My mum had a baby girl when I was 3 who died in childbirth. I was at the hospital in a corridor with Dad and they wouldn't let me see my sister because she was born dead. I heard my mum screaming and crying. Dad gave me to a nurse and went in to Mum. Then my gran (Mum's mum) came and took me home where she said I would have to be extra good to look after my mum and dad because they were going to be sad for a long time and my sister was born with lovely curly hair and looked like my dad, unlike me.

I wasn't allowed to the funeral. I hate my dead sister for spoiling my life even though you are not supposed to hate dead people, let alone innocent little babies. Her name is Cara.

This essay is short but I am tired. I have just played a football match which we won 3–0. I have no more words to say on this subject.

Teacher's Comments:

Adele, please arrange a time to see me about this essay.

CHAPTER 1

ENGLAND STARDOM AWAITS

The jostling on the touchline gets worse. Parents are still trying to get autographs off Faye White, the famous England football player who's scouting for England U15s. There are only two players on the pitch who can get picked for England – me and Mikaela. Most likely Mikaela will bag the place because my mum and dad were shouting all through the night last night so I couldn't sleep and I'm now dog-tired. I didn't even do my eyebrows this morning, I got up so late. I just scrunched my hair into a pony tail, applied some lippy then jumped in a taxi to the match.

It's 0–0 and Mikaela is doing her show pony thing. Everyone gives her the ball and she passes it out to the wingers, who pass it back. She then passes it between the midfielders, who pass it back. She does each move ballerina style, on her toes, every move fully extended. Showing off. The only thing she's not doing is passing it to me. I'm waving like a Bieber fan who's just spotted Justin at the airport, and Mikaela's completely ignoring me, going for glory on her own. *Enough,* I decide. I pull off my hair tie so my hair flows loose. I always feel freer playing like this, even if Miss Fridge says it's against the rules. I feint to run past Mikaela but instead nick the ball off her toes. *Now watch me go.* I leap over a tackle, spin round three other Bestwood Academy players, shimmy past the goalkeeper and tap the ball into an empty net. 1–0. Miss Jones (or Miss Fridge as we call her because she's cool and shaped like a fridge) is dancing on the touchline. Parents are whooping and clapping. Faye smiles right at me. I take a bow. I'm bathed in starlight. A girl could get used to this. Everyone in our team runs over to congratulate me. Everyone, that is, except Mikaela.

Mikaela mouths *bitch* at me. From the restart, she doesn't give me a single pass. Ever. After ten minutes of this, I stop running, tie my hair back up and look over to the touchline. Faye is still signing autographs. That will be me in three years' time, I dream. Gold earrings. Latest Louis Vuitton handbag. Red heels. A modelling contract with L'Oreal. Trophies spilling out of my cabinet.

I see something on the touchline that spooks me. A policeman. He's staring right at me. My heart lurches. I think about the crazy thieving I've done, nicking perfume, jewellery, sunglasses, purses, you name it. Am I going to get handcuffed in front of Faye White and led off the field in shame?

I wander across to the far touchline and free my hair again, slip my socks down to my calves and smooth my hands over my thighs. These legs are not only smooth, they're silky fast. If the cop makes a move, I'll outsprint him, I'm sure. Of course if they've brought a police dog, I'll give up instantly. I'm not having my legs torn up by some

8

psycho police Rottweiler. I look over at him again.

The cop shouts. 'Go, Jessie! Go girl!'

Suddenly everything's OK. He's just another pushy parent.

At half time it is 1–1. Miss Fridge tells Mikaela to get the ball to me more often.

'How can she score if you don't pass, Mikaela?'

Mikaela shrugs, flicks her braids out of her face then crosses her arms. She's wearing brand new, pink Nike boots, and she's flicking her feet to make sure everyone's noticing them.

Faye White comes over and puts her arm around Miss Fridge and they move away. Faye White definitely points at me, then Mikaela.

'Faye, Faye, show us some of your skills!' I shout out after her.

She shakes her head and points to her classy red heels.

'Oh, go on!' I kick her the ball.

Faye flicks the ball up to her head, does a spin turn while the ball's still balanced on her forehead, then lets it drop. She back heels the ball to me then says, 'No more, Adele. Another time, girls!'

I'm awestruck. Faye White knows my name.

'Tell! Tell! Tell!' everyone yells at Miss Fridge once Faye White has left. 'What did she say about us?'

'The prize is within your grasp,' says Miss Fridge to us all. 'Adele, she said your last goal "would have made Pele swoon".'

'Who's Pele?' I ask.

'Only the greatest striker who ever lived,' says Miss

9

Fridge. 'And Mikaela, your control, your passing. "Beckham would kiss your boots", she said.'

'She never said that in a million years. But still I'm all ears!' Mikaela pulls her ears to show Miss Fridge that she is all ears. It's funny. I laugh, even though Mikaela is a bitch for not passing to me.

'OK, enough, Mikaela. Do your rhyming on the pitch. And Adele?'

'Yes, Miss?'

'Concentrate. Get the ball. Then stick it in the net. Simples. Mikaela. Pass the ball to Adele.'

'What the feet don't know, the mouth can't tell.'

'Just do it, Mikay,' snaps Miss Fridge, sounding suddenly like a Chihuahua that's sucked on a helium balloon.

Mikaela gets the ball and fires it at me hard and fast. She forgets I have an older brother who smashes the ball at me like that every day. One touch and the ball turns from a cannonball into a feather. *Watch me go. England team here I come.* I weave round one defender, spinning away so tightly she falls on her bum. The goalie tries to crowd me but I feint to shoot left, then shoot right. The ball rockets into the net. *As easy as painting my nails.* I mime painting my nails just so they all get the point on the touchline. Everyone's all over me. I love it. Even Mikaela high fives me.

I dash upfield again. Mikaela plays a peach of a pass to me. It drops soft as a cotton bud onto my left thigh. I trap it then do a neat little chip shot. The ball spirals over the goalie, kisses the post and rebounds into the net. I do my nail polishing again.

Everyone's patting me on the back. Faye White is

clapping. *If that doesn't get me into the England team nothing will.*

Bestwood don't want to play anymore. Every time we pass the ball all the parents on our touchline are shouting *Olé!* When I say all the parents, that's all except mine. My dad only goes to MTB's matches. Mum came to a match once. She stood on the touchline, drunk. I scored but it was ruled off-side. Mum ran onto the pitch to try and punch the referee. Luckily, she tripped and fell so the punch missed. Miss Fridge carried Mum off, firefighter style. I told my mum never to come again.

The final whistle blows. Me and Mikaela are shattered. We're flopped on the pitch, leaning on each other, panting. All we really want to know is: who made it onto the England team? We're gathered around Miss Fridge.

'Faye White has left early to get up the motorway,' Miss Fridge says, 'but she left me this.' Miss Fridge waves an envelope.

'Come on, spill the beans, Miss, who's da Queens?' yells Mikaela, back in rap mode.

'What did Faye White say?' I chip in, translating.

'Inside this envelope is the answer,' Miss Fridge says. She slowly pulls out a piece of white paper, which she unfolds. 'Your whole team played fantastic,' Miss Fridge says, reading from the paper.

'Who? Who? Who? Who?' everyone yells.

'Wait for it!' Miss Fridge shouts over us.

We're all there, waiting.

CHAPTER 2

THERE'S ONLY ONE ADELE VIALLI

Miss Fridge moves her finger along the paper to read the note from Faye White, like she's five years old or something. 'She gave Mikaela Most Valuable Player,' she declares.

Mikaela jumps right up in a tail-shake dance. 'I'm on the England team! Dream! Dream! Dream!'

'I score a hat trick and I'm not?'

'Adele, stop sulking.'

Miss Fridge keeps on. 'Nobody's on it yet. Mrs White said she needed to see a few more matches. Now let's celebrate. We're in the Semis. Off you go, girls. Showers. Training's tomorrow. Nobody be late. Remember – you can make it into the England team if you train hard. No more late arrivals, Lucy! No more sloppy performances, Sid! No more daydreaming in the middle of the pitch, Adele!'

I trudge back to the dressing room with the rest of them. I was sure I was going to be picked for England. I scored a hat trick. What's a girl got to do?

Mikaela's dives into the showers and does this awful warbling. I imagine wildlife for miles around fleeing. She is Rhianna, without the talent or the looks. She gets the others to join in. I scrub up, spin out of the showers and start pulling on my clothes.

After ten minutes, Miss Fridge cuts off the water. There's calls of 'No, Miss!' and 'I only just got in!' and 'I'm still soapy!' Miss Fridge pays them no attention. She waddles back into her little changing room office, picks up her headphones and goes back to Skyping her mum, like she always does. Someone turns the showers back on. They're singing my praises now in there. I'm the hat trick hero after all, not Mikaela.

'There's one and one only! Adele Vialli!'

CHAPTER 3

MAMA MIA

I'm walking to the bus stop. I think a little bit about Miss Fridge. Yelling on the touchline. Throwing all the kit into the store room with one easy flip of her arm. Maybe she used to be a shot-putter? Then I'm thinking, *why does Mikaela not pass me the ball more?* It doesn't make sense, I'm the leading goal-scorer by far. Then again, not much about Mikaela makes sense. Still, she's my best friend.

Five Random Thoughts:

- Do squirrels ever eat anything other than nuts?

- If people have been dying for millions of years, where are all the bodies?

- Why do birds sing?

- What is it like to be a boy?

- Will I ever score in a World Cup final?

I catch the bus. As I get closer to home, I start to feel

queasy. It's always like this going home on a Saturday after a football match. It's the not-knowing that gets me. Will Mum be conscious? Will she be sober? Mum's always worse at weekends. Dad's never there. He's out at MTB's matches or then busy on business. When MTB does get home, he whizzes straight up to his room and does whatever boys do in their rooms with their door locked and music blasting. Everyone leaves all the worrying about Mum to me.

I get off the bus. Thoughts skid around in my brain. Each thought is worse than the one before. I imagine my mum drowning in the bath. I imagine her standing in the middle of a road, swaying, drunk. I start running. My phone goes off. It's Mikaela. She's texted me. I stop and get my phone out.

Well done, hat trick grl. ❤❤

I text her back.

Thnx gf u were brill 2 ❤❤

We do a snowball of best friend texts. Suddenly I'm not alone.

Why is Mikaela my best friend? We are total opposites. I'm thin, she's chubby; I'm tall, she's short; my hair's straight-ish, hers is tight, black curls. She's close to her mum, I never do anything with mine. I've got a boyfriend, she hasn't. She can name the capital city of every Caribbean Island in ten seconds flat, I can name the street that every Nando's in town is on in ten seconds flat. My skin's olive, hers is ebony black. Yet we're best friends. Why?

Five Reasons Mikaela Is My Best Friend:

☺ SHE KNOWS WHERE TO FIND ME WHEN I'M HIDING

☺ SHE CRIED WITH ME WHEN MY RABBIT DIED

☺ SHE LETS ME COPY HER HOMEWORK

☺ SHE'S FUNNY, LIKE WITH HER RHYME STUFF

Finally I reach home.

I put my key in the front door and open it. MTB rushes out. I head upstairs, drop my football boots in my boots bucket in my room (it soaks the mud off), then head across to my mum's room. Mum is on her bed, face up, eyes closed, mouth open. There's a swampy smell in the air so she's been smoking cannabis. Mum has various positions on her bed depending on what state she's in. The foetal position, with her knees hugging her chin means she's in her 'I lost my baby ten years ago and I want her back' state. If she's lying on her back with her hands clasped to her forehead, she's in her 'pity me, the neglected housewife' mood. If she's in the middle of the bed with all four limbs spread out starfish style then she's in her 'I've taken too much medication' mode.

Today she is face-up starfish. I watch her chest. It rises and falls. Under the swamp smell there's a stench. Where did she throw up? I get a mop and clear up the sick from the side of her bed. The bedroom floor is marble. Perfect

16

for cleaning up sick. I get a wet cloth from the bathroom. I sit Mum up, make her drink some water and wipe her face. All the while I'm thinking, *why can't my mum be normal?*

'Adele, darling, I'm not well,' Mum says, slipping back into her starfish pose as soon as she's gulped the water.

I imagine kidnapping her and leaving her on a desert island with no drugs or drink. That would cure her.

'You want me to phone a doctor?' I ask.

'No, I'll be OK. Your dinner's in the freezer. Microwave for twelve minutes.'

My dinner has been in the freezer for the last three months. I could be a taste tester for Iceland Foods.

Another flashback comes to my mind. Mia the housekeeper. Mia always used to smother me in her arms when I came home from school. Mum says I'm too old for that, but sometimes that's all I want, just a moment when I don't have to be strong. Mia was more of a mum to me than Mum. Cooking? Mia. Laundry? Mia. Putting the clothes away? Mia. Tidying up? Mia. Knowing where things are? Mia. Trying to keep the family calendar in the kitchen up to date? Mia. Saying 'hello, how was your day?' when I come home from school? Mia. Asking how was the match? Mia.

First Mum changed Mia's hours so I didn't see her, then she stopped her coming at all.

'We won, Mum,' I say. 'I scored a hat-trick.'

'Isn't that marvellous?' Mum says, sounding bored. 'Your brother's home.'

'He just left, actually.'

MTB can do what he likes. "Because he's a boy". I'm the one who has to stay in all the time. OK, I'm fourteen, but everyone knows girls are more mature than boys, so a girl of fourteen is equal to a boy of fifteen, if not better. Girls are more sensible. End of.

Mum groans. 'Men are vipers. You take them to your bosom and they sting your foolish heart.'

'Have you've been reading Shakespeare again, Mum?'

'Don't be cruel, Adele. More water.'

She sits upright for the water. I'm fascinated by her hair. Even with her bed-head on and bits of sick in it, my mum's hair is so shiny.

I stroke it. 'Have you always had beautiful hair, Mum?' I ask her.

Mum nods then rambles. 'It was the first thing your dad noticed about me. When I was pregnant with you, we had this tiny house and me and your dad would sit with our dinner on our knees, and you could touch all the walls from the sofa and he'd stroke my hair. I made your dad go out and get me a chicken biryani and when he got back I changed my mind and wanted pizza instead. We laughed and laughed – nothing was too much trouble for him then. We had nothing, but we had everything. Now we have everything and yet we have...'

She doesn't finish her sentence.

'What about me, Mum? You've got me.'

'Of course. Tony and you.'

'Did Dad get you the pizza in the end then?'

'Yes, he had it delivered – said I'd have less time to change my mind. Quattro Frommagy it was. Bellisima. He was teaching me Italian then. My own private Italian lessons. This freckled face girl from Skelmersdale learning

Italian. I didn't know he hardly knew any more Italian than me. But it was fun. Our own secret language. Per favore. Pono la mano qui. Bailare...'

'That sounds Spanish, Mum.'

Mum sails on with her story. 'And we drank Chianti... I had a florists shop back then and I was thinking of getting another one.'

'Why didn't you?'

Mum chases a fly of a thought. I wait patiently thinking maybe it's the drugs. Finally she catches it.

'Your dad got the bank job and he said there was no need ... he was earning a huge salary. I guess he was right, it's just I...'

Mum's voice is slowing down. I take the glass out of her hand.

'You what, Mum?'

She's fallen asleep. Her mouth hangs open with words on the edge of her tongue. I lie her back down on the pillow and go to my room.

And cry.

I'm not sure what I'm crying about. I've learned when I cry it's not always the obvious thing. Like you might think I'm crying because of the state my mum's in. Or because nobody in my family gives a stuff that I'm actually a star football player. Or because we're rich and maybe we would be better off poor. Or because I'm a girl and I would have been better off a boy. Or maybe it's none of the above and actually I'm lonely. By the way, I never cry. Adele Vialli does not cry.

CHAPTER 4

ADELE VIALLI, GREATEST JEWELLERY THIEF ON EARTH

Ten minutes later, I'm done with the whole runny nose and red eyes spectacular.

I find my Player of the Season Trophy from last year and I run round my room waving it, imagining the headline: *Adele Vialli Scores World Cup Final Hat Trick*. In my undies drawer, I count seven silver bracelets. Freshly robbed. Holding them in my hands feels good.

I put them back, lie on my bed and look at my phone. The light in my room has faded. It's almost night. I wait and wait and wait. Then I give in and text Marcus.

I hate texting Marcus first. He should be the one texting me. Boyfriends are so thick. Marcus is one of my brother's football friends, though they hate each other's guts. My brother thinks I go out with Marcus to annoy him. It's a very good reason but I actually happen to like Marcus. I've got no talk credit. Marcus never has any either. Sometimes I prefer texts anyway. They're more mysterious. I text him.

Hi. Hows u?

Am good. And u

Been betta

Wassup?

Family. Friends. Personal stuff. Take yr pik.

He doesn't text after that. I wait two minutes then I text him again.

Wot u doin?

Maths homework

Bit late 4 that?

True. Long story. Will txt u 2moro. Bye x

I give him a bye and a couple of kisses but I'm not impressed. What use is a boyfriend if he's more interested in his maths homework than your gorgeous self?

So I text Mikaela.

She phones me back straight away.

'Hi Mikay,' I say.

'What's wrong, star?' Mikay says.

'You ever watch them cartoons where the cat's running and it runs right off the edge of the cliff, and then there's this moment it hangs there, then it falls down in a blur?'

'Itchy and Scratchy.'

'One minute I'm a football superhero, then I come home and whoosh – the grounds all gone and I'm smack on the floor.'

'What's going on?'

I sigh. 'I'm coming home thinking, "has my mum taken an overdose today?" You know what that does to my heart?'

'Is she OK?'

'She's OK now. But what about tomorrow? Or the day after that?'

'One day at a time, innit?'

'I'm still shaking, Mikay. I can't even hit the buttons on my phone, I'm that shaking.'

'Listen, Adele, it's totally unfair what you're going through.'

'I don't know what to do.'

'Why is your mum so sad?'

'She found grey hairs in her fringe. And in her pubes!' I giggle.

Mikaela's silent.

'She had me pull them out.'

'You plucked hairs out of your mum's pubes?!'

'Nooo! Her fringe!'

'OK ... she's sad. Get her a bottle of hair dye,' Mikaela says. 'Is your dad going to be back soon?'

'I don't know.'

'You did the right thing. It takes a village to raise a child.'

'What do you mean?' Mikaela often has these sayings. If it's not the rhymes it's the sayings.

'You have to face backwards before you can face forwards.'

'Still not with you, Mikaela.'

She laughs. 'If you want, I'll come round and sleep over at yours, or you can sleep at mine.'

'Mikay, you're the best. You've got me crying now.'

'Don't, cos you'll start me off too and I've just put on mascara. Properly this time, before you start.'

'I'll be alright.'

'I'm going to leave my phone on under my pillow. Ring me any time and I'll pick up, I promise.'

I can hear an argument downstairs. Dad must be back. 'Mikay, I'm going now. But...thanks.'

'Stay strong, sister. Who loves ya, baby?'

'You do, Mikay. I love you loads back.'

I put my phone down. I don't know whether to believe Mikaela when she says both her parents were members of the revolutionary black music and protest group called the Black Panthers, but she talks good, fighting talk.

The shouting downstairs is getting worse. Something gets thrown against a wall. It makes a thud. I drag myself off my bed and go downstairs. At the foot of the stairs I stop and listen to the word tennis:

'This is your idea of getting ready?'

Dad.

'Why should I have to entertain your work friends?'

Mum.

'You don't get it do you?'

Dad.

I sit on the steps and listen it out.

'How can my saying, "what a lovely sausage roll you

23

serve, Mr Chateauhoffer" get you a big contract?'

'That big contract could save our bacon, girl. We're sinking, Zowie, we're going under. The house, the holidays, the jewellery, all gone if something doesn't arrive soon.'

'I never liked this house anyway.'

'You want to live in a field? Wake up, Zow. Are you even listening?'

'Say your car's broken down.'

'You stupid...'

I step in. 'Dad, Mum, say hello to your beautiful daughter!'

They turn, shocked. As if it has only just occurred to them that yes, they have a daughter and yes, she does actually live with them, and yes, she has ears.

'Not now, darling.'

They both say this, and at exactly the same time.

Dad's holding an ornament. It's a black swan and he's got it by the neck, about to chuck it at Mum, who is by a door ready to duck behind it. Dad is dressed up in a blue velvet suit. He's had a haircut. Mum is barefoot. On the carpet is the wooden flower bowl and the flowers that were in it are scattered all over the floor. When Dad threw the last flower bowl the glass shattered everywhere, so Mia replaced it with a wooden one.

'Your mother and I were having a little conversation,' says Dad, like they've been discussing the weather. He puts the swan back on the mantelpiece.

There's a beat during which they figure out I am not going to leave the room until they've sorted out whatever it is they are arguing about. Dad cracks first.

'She always does this to me,' he says, exasperated. 'I tell her way in advance, she agrees, and then last minute she's not ready or she's ... drugged up.'

'You told me it was next week.'

'This week.'

'Next week.'

'Dad, why don't you check the date?' I say.

'It's in my phone,' says Dad, 'It's...'

Dad is scrolling through his phone. He stops on some page. 'Oh,' he says.

'So you messed it up, Dad?' I say.

'In my phone it's next week, but it got changed and... What does it matter what week it is, your mum's not doing anything tonight is she?'

'Talk to Mum, not me. Nicely.'

'What do you mean, "nicely"?'

'Say please. And like the dress she chooses.'

Mum is loving this.

Dad swallows hard. 'You were right, Zowie,' he says, totally grovelling. 'I told you next week and I was wrong, it's this week. Please. Will you come?'

'Pretty please?'

'Pretty please.'

'I'll consider it.'

Mum swans upstairs.

Dad fumes.

'She's going, Dad. She's just torturing you for a little while, but she's going.'

'Are you sure?' Dad asks me.

I nod. I pick the scattered flowers up and put them back

in the bowl. 'Have you eaten?'

'No,' says Dad, distractedly.

'Go and eat something then.'

Dad goes into the kitchen.

Later, after they both leave, I find Mum's vodka. It's vile. Everything is pretty much a blank after that.

I wake up to music. I can just about make out the clock on the wall. It says 2 something am. I'm on the sofa. Some old-time music is playing and Mum and Dad are dancing slowly in the room, chewing each other's face off. Mum's dress is beautiful and looks like it's about to drop off. Dad's trying to help it on its way. I push myself up off the sofa.

'Eughh! Mum! Dad! Get a room!' I say.

They carry on with the face-chewing like I'm not there.

I haul myself to my feet and stagger up to my bedroom.

MTB knocks and comes into my room. I guess he stays up as late as me nowadays. He sees my boots bucket and asks the score and says well done, even puts his arm around me. But I'm mad at him for not tidying up, for not looking after Mum (he says he hates cleaning up sick and why should he?) and for, well, being my brother. I kiss him anyway then tell him to get out and let me sleep.

Lying back, I imagine myself in five years' time. Will I be *Adele Vialli, Greatest Football Player on the Planet*? Or *Adele Vialli International Jewellery Thief*? I hear Mum and Dad stumble up. I'm half awake, half dreaming. Boys say girl footballers are all lesbians, but girl players have got hot bods. Faye White got a medal from the Queen. Her Majesty had better get a red carpet ready for me! I imagine the Queen and me having a kick-about at Buckingham Palace.

CHAPTER 5

BLACK BOYS & ITALIANS

I'm in Dad's car on the school run.

'I saw that Marcus play yesterday,' Dad says. 'Scored and ran the game. Smart player, Marcus. Your boyfriend.'

I say nothing, just wait for it. Marcus must have played against MTB and made him look average. I hide a smile.

'Why don't you go out with a good Italian boy?'

I knew it. 'There are no Italian boys,' I say. 'We're not in Italy. You mean good white boys.'

'It's not that he's black,' Dad says. 'It's that he's what do you call it? Ghetto. He lives on a council estate. Those places are full of thieves and dealers and gangsters...'

I turn on my phone and bring up a game. Sometimes I can't be bothered to answer my dad, he's so prejudiced.

Dad keeps on. 'It's like you don't even like your own people,' he says. 'You should be proud to be Italian. Or white.'

'It's not me having the identity crisis here, Dad. Marcus is not a black boy. Marcus is a boy. And I happen to like him. Anyway, your own mum was black.'

Dad looks at me finally. 'What gives you that idea?' he says.

'You showed me her photo, remember? I said she looked dark, and you laughed and said that's because she was part-Egyptian.'

Dad laughs again. 'Ethiopian. She did say her father was Ethiopian, but I don't know. She didn't talk about it much.'

'Doesn't that make you and me black?' I ask him.

Dad laughs. 'It makes you and me Italian!'

I'm fed up with Dad again. He twists everything. I concentrate on playing the game on my phone.

'Got out the wrong side of the bed, did you?' Dad says after a bit.

'My bed's against a wall. I get out the same side every morning.'

'Metaphorically.'

'Shut up, Dad.' I make out I'm texting so Dad can't talk to me anymore. For once, the school gates can't arrive fast enough.

There are thirteen reasons why I don't like school. They are (in no particular order):

Official titles:	*What I call them:*
Maths.	*Boring*
Maths II.	*Double Boring.*
English.	*What Ho Forsooth*
Biology.	*Body Bits.*
Chemistry.	*How To Blow Things Up.*
Physics.	*How To Electrocute Your Brother.*
Art.	*Ear Choppers.*
History	*Old Stuff.*
PSHE.	*Why To Persuade Boys To Wear A Condom.*
French.	*Adieu.*
German.	*Mein Gott.*
PE	*Faster! Higher! Sweatier! F✱✱k Yeah!*
Remedial.	*Let's Bring The Mad, the Bad and the Plain Confused Together In One Classroom And Watch What Happens.*

I walk into the school grounds, my head still throbbing from arguing with my dad.

CHAPTER 6

MIKAELA MY FRENEMY

Sometimes Art is good and sometimes it's feeding time at the zoo. Today it's OK. After a boring lesson about pointillism, Miss Dolphin allows us to paint flowers using little sponges. Stuff soon starts getting flicked across the room. By the time Miss puts dolphin music on, half of us are on our phones. I have a pic of Marcus on mine as my wallpaper. Mikaela sees it.

'Who's that?' she asks. I can hear the jealousy in her voice. I sigh loudly to let her know that I know she's gaming me.

'He's fit,' she says. 'You got the pic off Facebook. Your imaginary boyfriend is it? Give it here.'

She grabs my phone off me. 'Nice,' she shouts, 'a black boyfriend to go with your black gran.' She starts waving my phone at the whole class. 'Look! Adele Vialli is surrounded by imaginary black folk!'

Afterwards everyone asked me why. Answer: *she shouldn't have dissed my gran.*

I grab her hair and she grabs mine. Then she's wailing and thrashing on the floor. I cling to her.

'Adele, look what you've done, you've ruined her hair!'

Miss Dolphin is standing over us.

It's only as I push myself up from the floor that I see the clump of Mikaela's braids in my hand. I can't believe I've torn out so much of her hair.

'Off! Now! To Remedial! Immediately!' says Miss Dolphin, followed by, 'Mikaela, you poor thing!'

Mikaela is still on the floor, bawling and clutching her head.

I pick up my bag and start walking out of the class as instructed.

'Get back here!'

I turn to go back to my place.

As I turn, Mikaela rushes past me, still clutching her head.

'Not you, I meant Mikaela,' says Miss Dolphin to me. 'You, Remedial!'

I turn again and make the walk to Remedial. Why am I always the one to get the blame? I've had it up to here with Mikaela Robinson. Is it my fault she hasn't got a boyfriend? She is a sad, sulky, jealous bitch.

I really don't mind Remedial. They let you doze here, so long as you've got headphones on and you're listening to some Educational CD about something like the Fall of The Roman Empire. Everyone just whacks the volume down to zero and snoozes.

I wonder about Mikaela again, what's eating her. It's like my mum and dad when they argue. What they're arguing about is never what they appear to be arguing about. I decide she's trying to get the school to ban me from playing so she has more chance of getting noticed. She's sly like that.

The bell goes for home-time. I bundle everything into my bag and join the crowds fleeing for the bus stops. When I get home nobody's in, not even Mum. I imagine her staggering around outside an off-licence somewhere.

In the bathroom, I look in the mirror. There's a pink bruise above my right cheek and my lip is cut in one corner.

I fall asleep. I wake up in a panic, thinking, *I forgot to look for Mum.* I find her. She's back home, in bed, snoring.

CHAPTER 7

BENTLEYS & AFROS

Next morning as I walk through the main doors, I'm stopped by a Teaching Assistant who takes me to the Counselling Room. He tells me to sit with my legs together, keeping my hands visible at all times. He obviously moonlights at prisons. The Counselling Room is also the Sick Bay. I'm guessing Friday morning is Year 7's PE time because there's three Year 7 fakers in here, all holding their noses or clutching their stomachs, while grinning at one another.

I think about the war in the Middle East. I think about genetically modified foods and their effect on the food chain. I think about whether Beyoncé will ever split from Jay Z. I don't think about why I've been told to wait here because I know.

Miss Duras strides in. She runs Counselling, Sick Bay and Careers. A woman of many talents. She's got Mikaela tucked behind her. My mouth drops for a moment. Mikaela's hair is one huge Afro. I can't help giggling.

'Don't laugh, bitch. I'm gonna stab you!' says Mikaela, safe behind Miss Duras.

'That's enough. Sit down. Mikaela. Sit.'

Miss Duras orders all the 'ill' kids out into the corridor

so it's just us three, though I can see a Year 7 eye pressed up against the keyhole of the door.

'I thought you two were best friends. Adele, what's going on?' asks Mrs Duras.

'She keeps saying my grandmother's not black.'

'Is that true?'

'Her grandmother isn't black,' Mikaela sneers. 'She's white as Snow White.'

'Mikaela, if Adele says her grandmother is black then her grandmother is black. We believe in self-definition at this school.'

'It's just not expressed much in my genes,' I add for Miss Duras's sake.

'Well, there you go. So that's the end of it. Are we done?'

Mikaela speaks up. 'She says I'm not street. She says my dad drops me off in a Bentley and I live in a mansion not a council estate.'

'And is it true? Does your father drop you off in a Bentley?'

'No.'

I'm amazed. Mikaela's just told an outright lie.

'Adele, you should not say things that are untrue,' says Miss Duras. 'Nobody needs to be anything or anyone other than who they are. This school is a Harmony school. We have Asians, Chinese, Africans, Somalis, Greeks, Muslims, Polish and Roma here. We are more diverse than the United Nations. Everyone has to be proud of who they are and be happy with that. Understood?'

She says it like a threat. We both nod because otherwise Miss Duras will keep going with her speech. Unfortunately, she keeps going anyway.

'In this school, for some bizarre reason, black is seen as the height of cool. We can all speak Urban, *you get me?* But that doesn't make you black. Black is the traffic lights inventor, black is Mary Seacole, the Victorian nurse, black is the first astronomers, black is the Arabic maths, black is the Egyptian kyrogriphics.'

It's hieroglyphics not kyroglyphics, I think. But who am I to interrupt Miss Duras, mid-flow?

'...So you might both want to be black but if you want to be truly black you need to check out what black actually is. Black actually is going to your lessons and studying hard.'

'Are you gay, Miss?' says Mikaela. She has been looking at Miss Duras' thick eyebrows, lip-stick free lips and sports bra straps.

'I don't have to answer that question,' says Miss Duras without missing a beat.

'Miss is gay!' says Mikaela, astonished, then, 'That's OK, Miss. We'll keep your secret.'

Miss Duras gets back on her theme. 'So that was what you were fighting in class about yesterday?'

'That, and she says I don't have a boyfriend, when she knows I do,' I reply, 'She's just gaming me cos of the England team thing.'

Miss Duras is looking at her (quite manly) watch. The bell rings. She's out of time.

'Mikaela, whether Adele has a boyfriend or does not have a boyfriend is no concern of yours. Girls, we cannot have fights at school. Whatever the England thing is, be nice to each other. You will be in serious trouble if it happens again. Adele, look what Mikaela has had to do to her hair because you pulled her braids out.'

'I'm proud of my new hair, Miss,' says Mikaela, 'it's natural.'

'I wish I had an Afro,' I say, 'it's brill.'

'That's better, girls. Support each other. Now shake hands and let that be the end of it. Promise?'

Another threat. We both nod and shake hands.

'Go to your next lesson together, nicely, or I'll make your lives not worth living. Understood?'

I give a Year 7 a bashed head when I swing open the Counselling Room door. Serves the little sneak right.

CHAPTER 8

HOW TO SURVIVE PARENTS' EVENING

'Mummy, you really need to go to Parents' Evening.'

'Darling, I'm sure you're doing wonderfully.'

'But they want you to hear how wonderful I am.'

We're in the kitchen. I've just got back from school. Mum is looking for a tin of macaroni cheese to serve with toast as my tea. Mia would have cooked steaming Italian pasta in a homemade tomato sauce. Nevertheless, I smile at Mum. She's almost sober and she's making an effort. 'Thanks, Mum,' I say when she serves me. I kiss her. 'You're the best.'

I don't actually want my mum to go to Parents' Evening. I binned the School Report they posted last week and faked an email from the school to Mum. It said:

"We have attached your daughter's school report. Save trees by not printing this file."

In my version of the Report, I am Exceptional in all subjects except Maths (no point in pushing it too far).

Mum gets through about forty reasons why she's not going before I say, 'OK, Mum, I've got to do my homework now.' I leave her babbling something about orchids.

Later, Dad gets back and I hear him ask Mum why she accused the housekeeper of stealing her vodka and sacked her. The two of them then spin through their full set of other arguments.

The Complete Mum & Dad Arguments Playlist:

You Don't Love Me. (Mum)
Love Is Not Found In The Bottom Of A Bottle (Dad)
I've Got A Weak Heart (Mum)
Anything Microwaved Is Not A Meal (Dad)
Don't Fuck The Hired Help (Mum)
You Are Now Being Ridiculous (Dad)
I Can't Take This Loneliness (Mum)
I Work All Hours & It's Killing Me (Dad)
[Even If] You Were The Last Man On Earth (Mum)
Nail Me To A Cross, It's Quicker. (Dad)

Dad then accuses Mum of internet dating. She says it's not dating it's a friendship site. Dad says why are all the people she has 'liked' on the site men, then? Mum says they're not, it's just those are the ones he noticed and anyway why can't she have male friends? Then they start kissing. I go into the kitchen and this breaks them apart but ends (by the weird logic only known to my parents) with Dad saying *he* will go to Parents' Evening and what's more he will take me with him. Disaster.

They start ballroom dancing together in the kitchen.

In the car on the way to school next day, Dad says he had not realised all these years that there's not one brilliant football player in the family, there's two. And that from now on, he is going to support me totally and he's ashamed he hadn't noticed earlier. He then leans over and kisses me on the cheek.

This is so unlike Dad I don't know what to say. I actually feel a drop of water escaping from my eye. I brush it away and mumble, 'Dad, I think that's the nicest thing you've ever said to me in my life. Ever.'

'Nicer than "OK, I'll buy you the dress"?'

'Way nicer.'

'I know Tony gets a lot of attention. But you're my daughter, and I love you to bits. Don't ever forget that.'

I'm having to dab my eyes again now. We're stopped at traffic lights. 'Are you feeling alright, Dad?' I throw him a look that is somewhere between a smile and an accusation.

He laughs, gets the car moving again. 'You're an enigma, Adele,' he says.

'You're not that good-looking yourself,' I tell him.

That gets him. He loves it. And I think, why can't me and Dad have good times like this more often?

'What am I going to hear at Parents Evening?' he asks, smiling mysteriously.

I sidestep the question. 'Mum wants you to dance with her.'

'What?'

'I mean not in the kitchen. Take her out dancing. Like when you first met her. She says you and her went dancing in clubs together.'

Dad moves off from the traffic lights in the wrong gear. 'I had some moves back then,' he says. 'We were good. It's strange. You have to run to stay still.'

'Taking Mum dancing.' I nudge him, because he's drifted off the subject.

'I would dance with your mum every day if I had the time. One decimal point wrong and you can lose the company millions. I've got all the Young Turks coming at me, eyeing my desk.'

'They're hiring people from Turkey?'

'No, it's an expression. Young, hungry guys, who want my job. They'd step over my dead body without a blink.'

Dad continues talking nonsense. I look him over. I guess he'll be OK at Parents Evening. It would have been better if he'd built up a bit of a suntan, then he would maybe pass for at least a bit Ethiopian, even if he's a long way from looking black.

In between humming a tune Dad says that, with the World Cup coming up soon, the big companies are looking for branding opportunities and they'll pay lots of money for girls who can do football tricks to be in their adverts. He has access to these companies through his bank.

'Bring them on!' I say, and he laughs.

We pull up in the school car park and I spot Mikaela. She's trying to hurry her mum away from their Bentley. I shout **'Hi Mikaela!'** really loud so she has to wave back. Her mum waves back too. She ushers Mikaela over to me. Her mum's in a push-up bra, her eyebrows are sculpted, and her pencil skirt holds her bum tight. Dad approves of all of it. I want to kick him. Dad kisses Mikaela's mum once on each cheek.

'Very continental,' Mikaela's mum says, blushing at

Dad's double kiss.

'Enchantay,' says my dad in bad French.

I roll my eyes. Old people never lose an opportunity to flirt. Like their lives matter anymore.

'Nice car,' I say to Mikaela.

She gives me the finger.

'Mikaela!' her mum says. She is walking ahead of us but somehow saw it.

'She just asked me what room's History, and I was saying Room One,' says Mikaela.

'That's very helpful of you, young lady,' my dad says, turning to Mikaela.

Dad and Mikaela's mum are highly amused by this, for reasons known only to old people, I assume. Before you know it, the two of them have decided to do the tour of teachers together, and drag us with them.

We do English, Maths and the Sciences, one after the other. Eventually, Dad manages to sit through the teachers' whingeing and complaining without shooting me 'You-are-dead-when-you-get-home' looks. Mikaela's mum has taken to patting him on the shoulder during each teacher's act of revenge on me and Dad likes this so much he's almost disappointed when a teacher says something nice and he gets no consoling pat.

'Only two more to go!' Mikaela's mum says, merrily.

Dad laughs out loud.

The art teacher, Miss Jobanputra (aka Miss Dolphin) forgets all my hard work in pottery and simply tells Dad about that one little fight. Dad says it will never happen again. Mikaela's mum butts in and says her daughter is as much to blame as me, then she goes on the attack:

'Have you heard of Emory Douglas?' she quizzes Miss Dolphin.

'Is he in my class?' Miss Dolphin asks.

'Emory, whom I have met in person, was the Black Panther's graphic designer,' Mikaela's mum lectures her. 'He did so much for positive images of black people. Are his design principles taught at this school?'

My dad, who has been a racist all his life (Dad's Racist Playlist: Islam Is The Cause Of All The World's Problems. There's Too Many Black Football Players. There's A Reason The Roma Are All Poor And Criminals. This Island Is Too Small.) is nodding fervently as Mikaela's mum makes her point.

Miss Dolphin faffs and stutters. 'We teach a wide range of influences,' she manages. She then smiles the way psychiatrists smile at crazy people (I guess) and taps her watch. Time's up for the two of them.

Mikaela pats her Afro proudly and her mum goes doey-eyed on her. Dad says, 'You have a beautiful daughter, and I can see where she gets it from.'

Mikaela turns to me and mimes two fingers down her throat at the same time as I'm doing the same action. That has us in giggles.

The last room is next to the toilets. It's PE. No parents are in there. Mikaela's mum wants to give it a miss – 'On principle, the stereotyping of black children as athletes is dreadful,' she says.

Dad agrees but persuades her to go in.

Miss Fridge reminds me of a drowning woman grabbing

42

for a lifebuoy. She seizes our parents and sits them down.

'It is a double honour to have before me parents of the two most exceptionally gifted football players I have ever had the pleasure of teaching in my entire career. They could both make the England team. Imagine that!'

Dad is impressed.

Miss Fridge is relentless: 'Mikaela is an amazing midfield general, Adele is a simply amazing goal scorer. If you two girls could play as a team, we could win the League. Imagine that! And have both of you playing for England!'

I can see my dad and Mikaela's mum are actually imagining this, Dad with dollar signs in his eyes, Mikaela's mum dreaming of Mikaela doing a Black Panther lap of glory, clenched fist held high.

'Unfortunately for us, nobody knows which of them is going to turn up on match days, whether Miss Jeckyl or Mrs Hyde,' says Miss Fridge. 'At England level, they're looking for consistency and I have to deliver my opinion on that to the selectors.'

'Consistency is no problem for my daughter,' says Dad. 'She gets out of the same side of the bed every morning. Very consistent.' This amuses both Dad and Mikaela's mum.

'What about you, Lydia?' Dad asks Mikaela's mum.

'I've brought Mikaela up to be consistent,' says Mikaela's mum with robot eyes.

'Consistency is what I shall need from these girls to show they are ready for England. And you, the parents, can help with that.'

Dad is startled, but loves it. Mikaela's mum takes it in her stride.

'As parents,' Miss Fridge says, poking towards them with a finger, 'you must want them to play for England. True?'

They nod.

'That means making sure they get to matches on time. And having a good night's rest beforehand so they are ready to *Give Their All*. With your help, as good parents, we can get a hundred percent from both girls at tomorrow's match.'

Miss Fridge would have gone on for another hour but a bell rings to indicate Parents' Evening is over.

'I'm sorry,' says Miss Fridge. 'Our Union says we must stop now. No overtime. We're in dispute. I'm sure you understand.'

On the walk back to the car park, Mikaela's mum says she totally approves of the teachers' position on unpaid overtime, and that workers can only win by acts of solidarity, anything else plays into the hands of the Capitalists, their Bankers and the other Oppressors. My dad agrees wholeheartedly and gets her telephone number 'as an act of parental solidarity' before Mrs Robinson and Mikaela get in their Bentley.

'Nice car, Mrs Robinson,' I say.

'Thank you,' says Mikaela's mum, sliding behind the wheel. 'And it's we women who need to be in the driving seat in this world. We've watched the men mess it up long enough!'

Dad chuckles. Mrs Robinson pulls off, then promptly stops again because her car is making a racket. She's got a flat tyre at the back. She gets out. 'Just my luck,' she says. 'I'll call the RAC.'

'That's an hour's wait,' says Dad. 'Could I...?' He gestures

44

to the wheel.

'You sure?' asks Mikay's mum.

'It's no trouble.'

'I could of course do it myself.'

'Of course. Maybe we should do it together?'

'That works for me.'

'OK, I'll just get the spare and then... Can you pop your boot open?'

Mikay's mum looks at him a moment, then says, 'For you only, Mr Vialli, I'll pop my boot open.'

'Excellent,' says Dad.

They go to the boot and together heave the spare tyre out.

'Roll the wheel over here, Mrs Robinson, if you would,' says Dad, 'while I fish around and find the jack.'

Moments later they are both huddled by the flat rear wheel. They've soon hauled it off. 'It's teamwork,' Dad says, as Mrs Robinson rolls the burst wheel away. 'Don't underestimate your own muscles, girls.'

Dad picks up the spare wheel from Mrs Robinson. 'You have beautiful nails, if I may say so, Mrs Robinson,' says Dad. 'Beautiful, and yet practical.'

Mrs Robinson looks over to me and Mikaela. 'Never forget there's an Amazon inside each of us,' she says, in lecture mode.

'What's an Amazon?' asks Mikaela with her bored face on.

'A very fit, strong woman. Like your mum,' Dad replies.

I get the impression that neither of the two adults are actually talking to us, they're talking to themselves.

Dad's grunting as he tightens the nuts on the new wheel with the jack. 'If the wheels come off in your life,' he says, between grunts, 'you just have to find the jack and slot them back on. *Semplice*.'

'Enough with the poetry, Dad. *Abbastanza*,' I tell him.

'The only Italian I know is Vespa,' Mikaela's mum says. 'Those little motorbikes. My first boyfriend had one.'

'Mum!' snorts Mikaela, 'Too Much Information.'

'*Vespa* means wasp,' says Dad. '*A-pe* would be better for you, Mrs Robsinson. –*A-pe Regina*. Queen Bee. You have bee-stung lips.'

'Dad!'

Mrs Robinson sniggers. 'Shh. Not in front of the children.'

The two of them then laugh together like this is the best joke in the world.

I look over at Mikaela. She's as *bleugh* as me about it.

'Dad. Stop flirting. Now!' I tell him.

'Sorry,' says Dad, although he's still enjoying himself. 'Just a bit of fun.'

The new wheel is on. Dad drops the damaged wheel into the Bentley's boot and Mrs Robinson and Mikaela get into the car. Everyone waves goodbye. A smile stays on Dad's face all the way over to our own car.

Then the Head teacher comes out and corners him. It's about unpaid school fees. Dad says there must be some mistake. The Head pushes some forms into his hands. Dad's face is lifeless when he gets into the car. He pulls out of the school grounds sharply.

'You hear what Miss Jones said, Dad? I could play for

England!'

This revives him. He starts nodding to some music inside his head. He says he's coming to the match tomorrow.

'Gre-eat!' I tell him. I wonder how much of his happiness is because of the England thing, how much is meeting Mikaela's mum again and how much is actually seeing his daughter play. Still, I'm happy that Dad's happy. He's been so miserable recently.

Later, Marcus doesn't pick up his phone or answer my texts. I ring his landline. His mum answers.

'Hiya, darling, he's not in right now love. You alright?'

'I may get on the England team,' I tell her.

'Ohmygod, Adele, magic! Well done!'

'I'm not on it yet,' I say, trying to calm her down as she oohs and aahs. She always makes me smile, she's so enthusiastic.

'You must be playing your socks off. Wait till I tell Marcus. Give yourself a pat on the back. I'm so proud of you.'

'Thanks, Mrs Adenuga.'

I press End Call and put the phone down. I have this lovely glow in my stomach.

Later, I get a text from Marcus.

Wel don. Mum told me. U da supernova star. Wil bel u 2moro.
Gotta sleep now footie 2moro x(()x

I text him back.

Me 2 xx(())xx

47

That glow in my stomach gets warmer. I think about Marcus. Why do I like him? Mikaela will say because he's poor and black and that bumps up my street cred. Actually, I like him because he's stronger and yet more vulnerable than other boys. I don't know if that's his blackness too. He's my first boyfriend and so how can I compare? His being black irritates Dad which is great, and me going out with him annoys MTB, which is even better. Marcus happens to be a star footballer. He even has a football nickname, The Silent Striker. He won the Manchester United apprenticeship over MTB, which made Dad furious. MTB begged me to not go out with him, but what girl ever takes dating advice from a stupid brother? There's something sad and unknowable about Marcus that makes me love him and want to be with him. Yes, every girl fancies him a bit. But he's mine, I bagged him. I know black boys take more shit than white boys from the police and that. Mikaela says that I'm stealing their men dem, that black boys are always checking white girls and it ain't right. Is it my fault though? And anyway, there's plenty of other black boys out there. She can check them, can't she? She shouldn't be going to war with me over my one boy. I flick through all the texts he's sent me and count the number of his kisses till I fall asleep.

CHAPTER 9

LEAVES & SHOWERS

It's Saturday morning at Hough End Playing Fields and as soon as I step out of the car, rain smacks my face. I look at the pitch. It's a lake. We're late. Dad shoves me into the changing room. Inside, everyone's moaning, nobody wants to play.

'My hair's going to be ruined!'

'I've got asthma!'

'I can't swim!'

'I wanna go home!'

Miss Fridge is fighting on all fronts. 'Mud? Mud is good for your skin,' she tells the wannabe Miss Worlds. 'And remember, it's the equivalent of two Detentions, but only if you play!' she tells the conscripts. 'Asthma? Stick your inhaler in your gob, girl, that's what it's for!' she tells the sick-notes. 'Think of the England places, girls!' she yells to everyone, finally.

As there's no escape, everyone starts to get their kit on. The gale must have got worse because from outside my dad shouts, 'I'm getting drenched, is everyone decent? Can I come in?'

He gets screams as a reply.

'No way!'

'I'm starkers!'

'Aaagh!'

Drama queens, all of them, I think.

'Poor thing!' Mikaela's mum says of my dad. She's been sitting in a corner of our changing room. She takes out a little silver compact, checks her lipstick, then leaves the dressing room to 'look after' my dad. I think, *yuk*.

The referee comes in. Everyone pleads with her to declare the match abandoned but she's having none of it: 'If eleven players are not on that pitch in two minutes I'll award the match to the opposing team! I've got a hundred essays to mark after this!'

The referee turns away. Mikaela calls out to her, 'Will you be issuing paddles, then, bitch?' Everyone cracks up at this. It's so not Mikaela.

The ref turns back. 'Who said that?'

We're all suddenly busy adjusting our socks. The ref looks to Miss Fridge. Miss Fridge shrugs that she didn't hear. The ref glares at Mikaela, but leaves.

We troop out. Dad dashes to the car park. When he comes back he's holding this huge golf umbrella that advertises his bank. Some touchy-feely argument starts up between Dad and Mikaela's mum about the umbrella. She's doesn't like the umbrella so she's attacking it and Dad's trying to fend her off. She catches the umbrella, points to the logo and wags her finger disapprovingly. Dad tugs the umbrella out of her grip.

Miss Fridge gives us a quick blast from the touchline. 'Mikaela, Adele, remember you're on the same team! Think

England!'

She couldn't have made it plainer. Cooperate or she won't write us up good. We're best friends again, as it happens.

Mikaela's mum is standing in the rain with an arm out to ward off Dad, who's spinning his umbrella, teasing her with it, inviting her to come under it. There are a few other parents on the touchline.

I get this flashback. My mum stumbling onto the pitch. Trying to attack the referee. I shake it off.

The referee holds the match up briefly while a bloke in a boiler suit tries to corner a stray chicken that has run onto the pitch. It flutters and squawks and soon has twenty four school girls chasing it across the field. Miss Fridge yells she wants to sign it up, which has us all laughing like crazy. It's a fast chicken, nobody can catch even a feather of it. Finally the boiler bloke dives and grabs it by a leg. He hauls it off upside down, still squawking and flapping. The chase has warmed us all up. Suddenly the conditions don't seem so bad. The match starts.

Mikaela collects the ball. She speeds away from two tacklers and passes it to me. I trap it under my foot, zip across the goal mouth and smack the ball to Sorayah who whacks it between the posts. There is no net so the ball sails all the way to the brambles by the disused railway line. Both teams and parents spend ages scrabbling around. When we finally find it, it's punctured and useless.

The other team starts yelling for us to abandon the match and half our team agree. But the referee marches off into the swirling rain and comes back with another ball.

I notice Dad has found a different, smaller umbrella

now, one without his bank's logo, and Mikaela's mum is huddled under it with him, even though the rain has stopped. It looks like they've linked arms.

Various parents are shouting encouragement from the touchline, making comments that only stupid parents with no idea how the game is played make:

'Awesome boot, Jemima!'

'Aim for the sticks, Helen!'

Only my dad shouts out anything that makes sense, mainly at me and Mikaela. My dad's got coaching badges in football.

Mikaela's on form. She's swinging herself into every tackle fearlessly.

Dad's abandoned his umbrella to Mikaela's mum and is running up and down the touchline, shouting at me. I love it. He usually saves all his hopping about on touchlines for MTB's games.

I score a beauty. With my back to the goal, I shoot it over my head. It flies into the bottom corner of the net. I do a gorilla chest-thumping slide into the mud that ends right at Dad's feet. Dad loves it, everyone loves it. The killjoy referee gives me a yellow card for time-wasting.

By the final whistle, all the players look like they've spent all week in a mud spa, but we've won 4–1 and I've scored twice. Mikaela gets Most Valuable Player Award from the referee and a warning that if she mouths off in a changing room at a referee again she will be banned for three matches.

Mikaela may have won Most Valuable Player, but yet again it's my name everyone's singing in the showers. I bow as the chants get going:

'Two, four, six, eight, who do we appreciate? Adele!'

'One, two, three, four who do you think we're shouting for? Adele!'

'We are blue, we are white, we are fucking dynamite!'

That one gets out before Miss Fridge can stop it. She laughs and lets it go.

'Three, five, seven, nine. Who do we think is really fine? Adele!'

'One, two, three, four. It's your mum cos she's a whore!'

'That's enough!' Miss Fridge says over all the laughter. She's happy though. Mikaela runs around for a bit showing off her Player of The Match medal. Then she comes up to me. 'You can have it if you want. After all, you got the goals.'

'I don't need it,' I say, 'I've got loads already.'

'Nah, take it.' Mikaela shoves it into my hand. Then she yells, 'Power To The People!'

Everyone joins in, yelling, 'Power to the People! Power to the People! Power to the People!' We're all so fired up we'll yell anything at all.

Mikaela's mum comes in and pinches her cheeks.

The showers have stopped working so everyone who didn't get in early has to go home in their kit, unwashed. I don't mind. When you've won, going home caked in mud is the best feeling ever. Mikaela is by my side as I finish packing.

'You want to hang out with me tomorrow?'

'What will we do?' Mikaela asks.

Her mum calls her over before I can answer.

Outside, my dad pats my back. 'You're incredible!

Brilliant! England Team's written on your forehead!' He plants a kiss on my forehead to emphasise this.

Sometimes I love my dad. After a couple more pats and a bit of a shoulder rub he says he has to head off to a meeting. Mikaela waves to me from her car as her mum drives her off. I catch the bus home. The drying mud feels good on my skin.

I get home, drop my boots in their bucket then check on Mum. She's awake, sitting in a chair in her room, with a giant, homemade cigarette in her hand. Curls of smoke drift round the room. She's gazing at the bedroom floor, which has leaves scattered on it.

'What's this?' I ask.

She raises an eyelid at me slowly, choosing her thoughts. The three lemons finally line up in her brain and she looks up triumphantly. 'I am contemplating Nature,' she declares.

'Have you made me anything to eat?'

'You're fourteen, darling, you can cook.'

'Bring back Mia,' I mutter.

'Pardon?' she says.

'Aren't you going to ask me if I won?' I ask her. I'm standing in front of her in full football kit, caked in mud and she still hasn't noticed.

'Careful where you step,' she replies. 'Those leaves are in a pattern.'

'Well?'

'Did you win?'

'Yes. And I scored two.'

'Well done you. Was your father there?'

'Yes. Flirting rotten with Mikaela's mum. Who was there

54

as well. Supporting her daughter. Like mums do.'

'Go shower, Adele,' mum snaps at me. 'You stink.'

I walk right through all her leaves which gets her yelling at my back.

In the shower I'm thinking, *I drew the short straw for mums.* Everyone says 'my mum is my best friend, we do our make-up together, we go shopping, we go to concerts, I help her choose her clothes, we go on holiday together, we do our Wii exercises together.' My mum does none of that. We do nothing together.

I go downstairs. Mum's come down and is watching TV. I go to lie on her. She pushes me off, saying she's too hot. I can smell vodka on her. She thinks vodka has no smell, daft cow.

'You ruined my leaf arrangement,' she says, slurring.

'It was a pile of mouldy leaves, Mum.'

'They weren't mouldy, they were green.'

'Right. Whatever.'

I get up and go into the kitchen and make myself a cup of tea.

Later that night I'm lying in bed and I think, my mum can dance. It's not very cool how she dances because her moves come from donkey's years ago, but she can move. I could teach her enough moves so she wouldn't embarrass me, then we could go to a concert together. What's the use though? She would probably say no. Her dancing partners (her partners in everything) are Lady Ganja and MC Vodka. Marcus's mum is more a mum to me than my own mum. And Mia was. I called Mia 'Mum' accidentally once, and Mum went mad. Some days it gets so bad, I want to scream at my mum but nothing comes out of my throat, like my windpipe's been cut. I just stand there, and she asks, 'what do you want?' And I say nothing.

CHAPTER 10

MC BANSHEE & HER GANG OF THIEVES

I text Mikaela early in the morning, then sneak out of the house before Dad can ask any questions. I know Mum will still be zonked from all her smoking.

At the Cheadle Park bus stop Mikaela gets on. She's wearing scruffy jeans. Her hair's flicked out into a full-on Afro again. She slides in next to me.

'What you laughing for?' she says.

'No, I love it, Mikay.'

'This fro's sexy like Beyoncé's backside. It's a black thing – you white folk won't understand.'

'My nana used to say that all the time,' I say. 'I be pinned tween her knees, and she sit there twisting her dreads and chewing hair grips between her lips, then sliding dem into mi head, going, "Black be God's colour. *Slide slide.* It be the sexiest, beautifullest. *Slide Slide.* Dopest colour in the rainbow! *Slide slide.* White people stupid what don't get that. *Slide.*"'

Mikaela laughs. 'What was that nonsene?'

'It's how my nana spoke.'

'Your imaginary nana! Who speaks imaginary bad patois!'

'She's dead now,' I say.

Mikaela shakes her head at me and pulls on her headphones, and I think, *Why did I just say that?* My nana was black, but I never met her. And she must have spoken Italian, not Jamaican. Sometimes I don't understand myself. I feel bad, like somehow I've done my nana wrong by pretending about her.

The bus fills up with the Saturday crowd of mums with kids, skateboarders and Goths. One guy gets on with a small plastic chair. He's the Statue guy that stands on Market Street in a big white blanket and white face paint.

'Look, the Statue guy,' I say, nudging Mikaela, who slides her headphones down to her neck. 'He stands dead still on a box. Then stretches an arm out and makes you jump. Like a beggar, but in a costume.'

'I got no time for beggars,' Mikaela says.

'You think you could stand on a lickle box all day?'

'I know you couldn't,' Mikaela says. 'You're attention deficit!' She laughs.

'Proper ASBO!' I agree. 'It's an easy rob though, Statues, if you think about it.'

'They're in the fuckin mafia. They'd break your legs, girlie.'

'Mafia don't travel on buses.'

Mikaela slides her headphones up again.

We get off the bus in the city centre and wait by the fountain.

It isn't long before MC Banshee arrives with Cakes. MC Banshee's boots kick the tarmac, her shoulders roll and her chin jerks around. Even the pigeons get out of her way fast.

'Who's she?' MC asks, when she gets to us. She jabs a finger into Mikaela's chest.

Mikaela flinches.

'A friend.'

'What's she doing here?'

'She wants to join.'

'I decide who's in,' MC says.

MC looks at me like she's deciding how far to push my nose into my skull with her fist. She's grabbed my jacket and is scrunching it up. It's starting to throttle me. She's smaller than me but she says she lifts weights every day and I believe her. I stay calm. She would have hit me already if she was totally mad at me, I reason, so this is for show.

'But you made me Chief Recruiter, didn't you?' I remind her, 'And Head of Research. And Specializer in Perfumes and Jewellery?'

It's the way I say it. All sweet and mild. Which is hard while you're being half-throttled. MC Banshee smiles, remembering. The dimple that sits in the middle of her chin comes up as she smiles. 'What's she good for then?' she says, releasing my jacket.

'She's sharp,' I say.

'I like your hair,' MC says to Mikaela.

'Th – thanks,' says Mikaela, trying to get her voice as low as possible. 'Your earring's nice.'

I go all air-hostessy. 'Mikaela, this is MC Banshee, this is Cakes. Together we are the South Henshawe Society of Shoplifters and Pickpockets. MC Banshee, apart from being leader, is also our Specialist in Trainers, Tops and Waterstones Books. Cakes is our Specialist in Gadgets and Edibles.'

'And vanilla slices,' adds Cakes.

'And vanilla slices,' I add.

'You got to eat,' Cakes explains.

Mikaela looks at me, as if to say, *is she really that thick?*

I look back at her with a look that says, *yes, she is, so get used to it.*

I continue: 'Our slogan is "a rob for one is a rob for all!" and we say the slogan every time we go nicking.'

'I say it first,' says MC.

'Go on then,' I say.

'A rob for one is a rob for all!' MC goes, putting her hand out as she speaks.

We latch hands together and then we say it with her. 'A rob for one is a rob for all!'

'What does it mean?' Mikaela whispers to me afterwards.

MC overhears. 'It's like licking blood,' says MC, 'or spitting into someone's mouth. You never been in a gang before?' MC Banshee eyes narrow, like she might punch Mikaela.

'Course!' goes Mikaela, scared shitless.

'Then shut the fuck up,' MC Banshee says. She wallops Mikaela on the shoulder, all friendly again, though she's no doubt left a bruise.

Mikaela asks me with her eyes, *is MC Banshee a nutter?*

I smile and shrug.

'Where are we doing?' I ask MC.

'Debenhams,' she tells us. 'Mary Poppins here can be the turnstile.'

'What's one of them?' asks Mikaela.

'Fuck,' says Banshee. 'What have you brought me, Magic?'

'I'll explain to her on the way,' I say.

We walk and I explain to Mikaela what a turnstile is. Basically the turnstile gets it from one person and gives it to another. It's the easiest job. The lifter takes the stuff, gives it to the turnstile, who gives it to the walker. The walker walks out with it.

'I don't want to be the turnstile though,' whispers Mikaela.

'Why not?'

'I'm black. I'll stand out.'

'Don't be daft. Look around. Hundreds of black people.'

'Why don't the lifters just walk straight out?'

MC is ear-wigging again. 'It messes with the cameras and the store detectives, innit,' she says. 'Even if we're caught they ain't got the right evidence. Now, are you in or are you off home to cuddle your Barbie?'

'What's everyone else doing?' Mikaela stalls.

'I'm lifting, so's Magic,' says MC. 'Magic's a walker, Cake's a walker. OK? I give to you, Magic gives to you. You swap them. Magic walks with what I lifted, Cakes walks with what Magic lifted. Got it?'

'What if they grab me?'

'Don't be fuckin soft,' MC says right in her face.

It's how MC explains things. Generally when MC explains things they stay explained.

'You've not left the store with nothing. Why would they grab you? Standing in a store aint illegal.'

MC rolls her eyes at me. We start walking in the direction of the shops. Mikaela nudges into me.

'Dell, is this what you've been doing Saturdays? It's so

fucked up. I don't want to do it. My mum would kill me.'

'Be cool, Mikaela. Nothing's gonna happen to you.' I squeeze her hand.

'I don't want to go to jail,' she blubs. 'They'd shave off my hair!'

'Nobody's going to jail, Mikay. Didn't you hear, MC? You're just stood there, doing nothing.' I'm speaking to her in my calmest voice.

'I won't make it to jail. Mum'd kill me first!'

'Mikay, get real. You're in a shop choosing a present for your mum. Anything goes wrong, you don't even know us, any of us. Understand?'

I get through this time.

'I don't know you. I've not nicked nothing,' she repeats.

With Mikaela chanting this, we catch up with the others.

MC takes one look at Mikaela and says. 'No way Mary Poppins's turnstiling, she's jelly. She can watch. Me and Cakes will go in by the Station door, Magic, take her through the Starbucks door and up the stairs. We'll meet in jewellery. Straight lifts.'

I give Mikaela a crash course in shoplifting on the Debenhams staircase. 'Right, Mikaela, when we go in there, don't be swivelling your head like a mad doll, yeah? Just watch out of the corners of your eye.'

'What for?'

'Store detectives. They're usually big blokes in jeans. They've got short hair and boring jackets, with a bulge where their walkie-talkies are. If you spot anyone watching us, you come up to me and say, "you've lost your bus fare". That means I should put back what I've lifted. "Through the keyhole" means there's someone spying on us and we should give up what we're trying to lift. Got it?'

Mikaela is still chanting, 'I don't know you, I've not nicked nothing,' but she nods.

We go into the store and Mikaela follows me around like Little Bo Peep.

'Mikaela, stand here and block me from the camera. Nice. Good.'

She does what I say quite well. She even manages not to swivel her head too much. She's still a bit obvious though. The jewellery is quite tricky. I have to shift Mikaela around three times before I get what I want.

I toy with doing sunglasses. You spin the carousel and keep trying on lots of sunglasses until the shop assistants and the cameras can't tell whether you're coming or going. If you arrive with a rubbish pair, you can then swap them for a good pair. The assistant is none the wiser because there's no gap in the carousel. You take the tag off in the toilets, then walk. Better still, if there's two of you, hide the sunglasses in the toilets. The other girl goes in, picks them up and walks them. If she gets stopped, she can just say she found them in the toilets, that's not theft. I could write a book.

I decide not to though. There's two blokes who don't look like they'd wear sunglasses nudging around the carousels close to us. They keep spinning but never try them on. While they are looking at us MC has shown up and is getting busy with Cakes. I wait a bit so all eyes are on me and Mikaela, then I move us two away. I can tell MC understands what I'm doing.

On the stairs, Mikaela is mumbling, 'Did you get something?'

I nod.

'What do we do now?' she asks, her head swivelling like an office chair.

'Calm down and walk out,' I tell her. 'Hold my hand.'

'No, I don't know you!' Mikaela says, shrinking away from me. 'I'm just out shopping. You stay here, I'm going out first. You're not with me!'

'Fine,' I say. The way Mikaela is, I don't fancy walking out with her anyway, she'd panic if she was with me and saw one of the Uniform guys who hang around the exits giving everyone the evil eye.

Not long afterwards, I'm pushing out of the Debenhams doors. MC is close behind me. You're meant to walk out calmly, but the moment MC gets outside, she runs like her knickers are on fire. Me and Cakes run after her, laughing our heads off. Mikaela plays catch up. MC says afterwards that she ran because one of the Security was onto us and she saved us, we all owe her big time.

We're in a city park. It's show time. MC shows a pair of Ray Bans and three diamante necklaces. Cakes shows a pair of pink leather gloves.

'Your turn, Magic. Show.'

I go into my pocket and palm out what I've lifted. Two gold bracelets.

MC doesn't say anything. She just smiles the way she smiles when she's really pleased with what you've lifted. The smile that shows her dimple.

'Real gold?' she asks.

'Would I lift anything else?'

'They're beautiful. Was it a swap?'

I nod.

'I didn't even see you,' says Mikaela.

I shrug. 'That's why I'm called Magic.'

MC grins. 'One each?'

'Course,' I say. '"A rob for one is a rob for all".'

MC kisses me on the cheek. Then her phone rings. It's a Mad Axeman ring tone. She and Cakes have to split. Mikaela takes off too, saying she has to meet up with her mum at ballet school in five minutes. Suddenly I'm on my own.

I catch the bus. When I get home, Dad's car is not on the drive. I open the door and immediately I can smell my brother's in. I go into my mum's room. She's not on her bed. I check the floor. She's not here. Where then?

I get a flash. *Mum drowning in a bath of vodka, with a line of lit spliffs in front of her on the plastic tray thing that goes across the bath.* I check both bathrooms. She's not in either of them.

She's not in.

I tidy up the kitchen, then go up to my room, jump on my bed, and toy with my new bracelet. I wonder where Dad is. I wonder where my brother is.

I decide to phone Marcus. I've got no phone credit so I pick up the house phone. Out of habit, I wait a few seconds to make sure MTB does not pick up an extension somewhere and listen in (he's done it before and I only caught him when he started giggling when I said 'bye bye, sweetie-pie, I love you' to Marcus), then I dial Marcus's house phone number. His mum answers.

'Hi Adele, he's out shopping for new shin pads. He got kicked rotten today. You OK?'

'Fine. Did he win?'

'Yes, love. He's on Cloud Nine. Happy as Larry.'

I can hear a child wailing in the background. Then Marcus's mum shouts: 'Put that down right now! That's enough! Now go and sit on the naughty step... '

The voice comes back close to the phone.

'Not you, Adele. Leah,' Marcus's mum says, half-embarrassed. 'It doesn't work, mind you. She has all her toys there, by her naughty step, she actually likes it. I'm so happy to have Leah, after all these years of boys. Finally I can get some pink in here.' She laughs. 'Did you have a match today, love?'

'No, yesterday.'

'How did it go?'

'We won. I scored twice.'

'Brilliant. Is the England team knocking for you?'

'They've not told us yet.'

'That's not "no" then is it? I'm chuffed for you. So proud of you, Adele!'

The way Marcus's mum says it, I can almost feel her squeezing me in an enormous hug of happiness over the phone.

'Thanks,' I say, blushing even though I'm on the phone.

'If Leah turns out half as good as you, I'd be so happy.'

'I'm not all good,' I say.

'Don't be like that, I mean nobody's perfect, I'm sure you're a moody cow at times like us all but you're a good girl, Adele, and I won't hear any different.'

'OK,' I say, giving in.

'And you make Marcus so happy. The way he beams when he talks about you. Don't tell him I told you, he likes to act all sad and moody, I mean he is all sad and moody, except when he talks about you.'

'He doesn't ring me much though, does he?' I say.

'No, he's not very good with talking on the phone. He prefers to text. You sure you're alright, Adele?'

'Yeh. I got to go now, start my homework.' I do a big groan.

'Sooner you start it, sooner it's finished, right? I'll tell him you called. Look after yourself, darling.'

'OK. Bye, Mrs Adenuga.'

I do that thing where I imagine I was swapped at birth and actually Mrs Adenuga is my real mum (except that would make Marcus my brother!). She so believes in me, she wants Leah to grow up like me. It makes me feel bad about the shoplifting.

I place the gold bracelet with the others. They look cool sitting all together. We've never been caught, though once this bloke chased us outside of Mango. We've never been to Mango since then.

I use my laptop to go on Facebook, Mikaela's Status Update says:

Had the most amazing time with Adele Vialli. Big up. The girl is Legend.

There's an attachment. It's a photo of what we lifted from Debenhams. *Shit.* I didn't know she took a photo. There could be girls from our school working at Debenhams who could recognise the stuff. I message her fast.

Mikay u idiot. Tek da fb foto down asap

Mikay's next Status Update opens.

4get wot I sed abt Adele Vialli. She is 1 big fk up. Just anotha Poor Lickle Rich Girl. Down With It? She dont know what It is. #Notanotherfaker.

Immediately three people jump in and a big argument starts with everyone insulting me or Mikaela or even random other people. Mikaela deletes the Status Update and all the comments tagged to it disappear with it. I'm about to message her, but my laptop crashes. I hear a curse. My brother puts his head round my door.

'How's little sis?'

'What's it to you?'

He shrugs. 'I've downloaded a virus and knocked out the Internet. Sorry.'

I throw my bedside lamp at him. It misses and hits the wall by the bookshelves, which crash into the mini fridge which sparks the socket and all the lights go out.

MTB disappears and two minutes later the lights come back on and he's back.

'Don't worry little sis, I've sorted it,' he says.

It's like he wants a medal for throwing a circuit breaker switch from Off to On.

'Good boy, well done,' I tell him, '*Dix points*. Off you go now, fuck off back to your own room.'

'Internet's still down though,' he says, lingering.

'You didn't fix nothing then, did you, baboon face?' I tell him sweetly.

He smirks. He actually likes it when I insult him. He's

hanging at my door.

'I guess now that all your sad hobbies are impossible 'cos the Internet's down, you've come to talk to me?'

'Something like that.'

I let him sit on the edge of my bed. I guess we're due a catch-up.

'You still wagging school now and then?' I ask him.

He nods. 'How did you know?'

'I tidy before I leave and you're a slob. When you're heading for the gym you always mess up the kitchen looking for cheese and leave it lying all over the place.'

'It's for my muscles,' he says. He flexes his biceps proudly.

While he's preening, I notice he's got flecks of mud in his hair, which reminds me he's played a match today.

'Did you win?'

His chest swells. '9–3.'

'Did you score?'

'Got Man of the Match, though.'

'Well done, you. Was Dad there?'

He shakes his head in an, *I-wasn't-bothered-though* kind of way.

Dad not being at an MTB match is unusual.

'Where's Mum?'

He shrugs again, this time with a flicker of concern.

'You eaten?'

'I'm not hungry.'

'Right. I'll make pasta a la Vialli. Buono?'

He grins a thank you.

As I go downstairs to the kitchen, I think, *my brother is not one of the world's greatest talkers.* The words get lost somewhere on the way from his brain to his tongue. But I do love him.

After we've eaten, we go out onto the front lawn and knock a football about. MTB is captain of his school team and a hair's breadth from being signed to Man United. Dad is handling the negotiations. MTB is better than me at tackling, but I can match him kick for kick otherwise. We're pinging the ball over the rose bushes when I hear the gates pull back and Dad's car pushing through the gravel.

We carry on playing to see who can hit the tallest rose first. I win. This annoys him and he makes it best out of three. When he loses that it becomes best out of five. We're on best out of thirty-one when Mum shouts us both to come inside.

MTB doesn't talk to me for the rest of the evening because I beat him. Which is great.

That night, under the covers, I'm still reliving my victory over MTB. How did I get so good? I remember how Dad put my brother into soccer coaching when he was six and dragged me with him. To shut me up, Dad would give me a ball to play with, a bright orange thing that had a string on it that attached to my ankle. (There's embarrassing photos of me wearing it). Whatever my brother was doing at training, I copied, like you do as a kid. I could juggle a ball five times in the air by the age of five. I got a pat on the head but I guess they expected that, being a girl, I would grow out of it. And maybe I would have if it didn't annoy MTB so much. Annoying your brother has to be up there with the best. 16–8 I beat him in our 'hit the rose' competition. I can probably even beat Marcus. My mind drifts. I hear Mum and Dad arguing downstairs but I don't hear any thuds so I don't go down and it goes quiet again. Marcus texts me goodnight with two kisses, which is one more than he usually sends.

CHAPTER 11

COUNSELLING IS CLOSED

Mikaela is in tears at Form Class this morning. Miss sends her to Counselling but Counselling is closed. Miss tells Mikaela she has exam-marking to do but she can see her at the end of school if she is still upset.

Mikaela slumps down next to me again and keeps up the sniffles. I've never known her so upset. I run through all my funny faces, even the ear pull trick, but she doesn't even notice.

We have double netball next and me and Mikaela are on different teams so I don't get to see her much but at lunch time I say to her, 'C'mon, let's sit somewhere and talk.'

We sit on a patch of grass at the back of the Science Block. She's looking at me like somehow it's me who's made her unhappy. So I take a guess.

'If you don't want to do the shoplifting anymore, it's no biggie.'

She curls her lip.

'I won't hate you if you get on the England team and I don't.'

She kisses her teeth.

'Help me out here then, Mikay. What is it?'

'I ... My ... I ... My mum and dad had this huge argument last night,' she says, tears streaming.

'Er. Excuse me? That's what parents do.'

'Now Mum's not taking me to Montego Bay this summer!' Mikaela's face is wet all over. 'It's not fair! We had it all arranged. Me and her was going to go together, we'd been planning it for ages. Now she's cancelled it!'

'That's cruel.'

'It would of been my first time in Jamaica. I would of met all the family.'

'How can she do that to you? That's your roots, what you always wanted.'

'And the beaches,' she sighs.

'Of course.'

'And the boys on the beaches.'

'And the boys on the beaches,' I sigh with her. I sneak a glance. She's sneaking a glance at me. We giggle. We can't help it.

'And all that spending money Dad was going to give me!'

'You'll get to go,' I say, trying to paint a nice picture for her. 'Maybe next year. Make sure your dad takes his credit cards if he's the one with the money.'

Mikaela bursts into tears again. WTF? I peel her hands from her face. 'Mikaela?'

She peers out through red-rimmed, cow eyes.

'What's going on?'

She wrenches her hands out of mine. 'You don't get it do you? My mum and dad are splitting up! Mum's having an affair. She's admitted it! Dad packed a bag last night and left

73

and now I have no dad! And no holiday with Mum!'

'Your dad's moved out?'

'It's sick, Adele, I mean, an affair, my mum? She's too old for sex. What's she doing having an affair? She's meant to be...'

'Playing Bingo with the old biddies at a Bingo Hall?' I ask.

Mikaela rolls her eyes.

'Taking her teeth out and soaking them in a glass at night?'

'She's meant to be sensible!' Mikaela says, thumping the grass. 'Sensible!'

'Listen, Mikaela, your mum's probably just a little bit confused cos she's getting old. It's called dementia. I read it on the Internet. The doctor gives them tablets and they think straight again.'

'She's not that old,' Mikaela sniffles, pushing my arm away.

'Then stop being daft. Parents argue. That's why they marry, so they can argue more. They'll get back together, all loved up. Then you'll be going for a month in Jamaica, not a week. Geddit?' I take her hands in mine. 'Say after me: "everything will be OK".'

I've only half convinced her. 'Everything will be OK,' she says, reluctantly, then, 'My bum's wet from the grass.'

'So's mine,' I say. 'Two wet bums.'

She smiles. The bell goes. 'Do I look like I've been crying?'

'Put some of my lippy on.' I dig it out for her. 'There. Ready for your photo-shoot again.' I haul her up. 'Now let's go to History and get bored stiff learning irrelevant stuff about what happened donkey's years ago to people that had no flushing toilets! Yeah. History! We love it! C'mon!'

We walk into History together. Except they've shuffled the timetable because a teacher is ill and it's not History, it's PSHE. *Good old PSHE*, I think. *Always the best lesson of any week.*

Personal Social and Health Education is taught by Mrs Amore Richards. To get Mrs Richards nickname we changed the first part of her name to Miss Loves because amore means love in Latin. And you are just going to have to guess what we changed the last part of her name to. Mrs Richards did Sex last week. Condoms. Cups and copulation. Diseases. Catholics. We all wet ourselves laughing. Sex, we learnt, is a squishy, serious, dangerous ting, like a bear parking a car on an ice floe. It happens between married adults who want to create a baby to save the world from under-population.

Everyone wants Sex again. Mrs Richards says we're doing Gender and Body Image. Somebody starts up a chant: 'Sex! Sex! Sex! Sex!'

Mrs Richards ignores us and puts a box on each of the five classroom tables. 'Do not open them yet!' she says. 'Who has any idea what Body Image means?'

Everyone gets their head down.

'Showering, Miss? Boys don't like to,' says the ever reliable Jennifer. She's on our table with Sorayah and Lubana.

'Good try, Jennifer, but that's body odour.'

'Women photographers, Miss?' someone from another table tries.

'Not quite. Let's find out then. Open your boxes and discuss the pictures inside among your group. Look at the pictures and make a list of what is real and what is unreal about these women. I'll walk round and give you some help if you need it.'

We open our box and dip in. 'Wow, that's a supermodel,' says Sorayah.

I read "Miranda Kerr" at the bottom of the photo. Miranda Kerr is wearing a bikini and is looking all slinky, pony-ing down a catwalk.

'I wish I had a body like that,' says Sorayah.

'She has got nice boobs,' says Jennifer. 'Like, a nice size. Real?'

We all vote yes and Jennifer makes the note.

'Perfect legs,' Jennifer says. 'Real?'

We vote yes again.

When we're done, we've all agreed Miranda Kerr in the photo is 100% perfect and real.

There's lots more photos in our box. We work through them. Most of them are really skinny.

'This is Beyoncé,' says Mikaela, pulling her out of the box. 'Don't nobody diss her!'

'What's not real about her?' asks Lubana, puzzled.

'She's wearing a weave,' whispers Mikaela, 'it's not her own hair.'

'Nooo! I don't believe you!' says Lubana.

'It's true. It's like the more beautiful you are, the more white you are, or the other way round,' says Mikaela.

'Fe true!' says Sorayah, suddenly dropping into Jamaican for a moment. 'My auntie uses skin lightening cream. She's

76

almost white now, but she can only afford it on her face and hands, so her legs are dark as mine.'

'I don't get it,' I say, 'why would your auntie want to look white?'

'So she's more beautiful.'

'I still don't get it,' I say.

'It's a black thing, Adele,' says Mikaela, 'you wouldn't understand!'

Mrs Richards shows up at our table.

'Who's that?' she asks as we look at a new picture.

There's no name on the picture and we don't recognise her. It's a leggy blonde in a one-piece bikini, with big hair.

'You are looking at the model, Cindy Crawford,' Miss says. 'You know what she said of herself? She said "I wish I looked like Cindy Crawford".'

'But she is Cindy Crawford, Miss,' says Sorayah.

'Exactly. Yet in this picture her legs have been made longer, her waist made thinner, and all her hairs and spots removed.'

Miss looks at our notes and frowns. We've decided everybody we've looked at so far is pretty much perfect and nobody is fake. 'I'll give you a clue,' she says. 'All these pics have been retouched in some way. Kate Moss isn't hairless. Angelina Jolie doesn't have perfect skin. Even Miranda Kerr doesn't look like that in real life.'

'But how can we tell, Miss?' asks Sorayah.

'It's difficult, isn't it?' says Mrs Richards. 'Have a go. Look more closely.' Then she goes off to another table.

Twenty minutes later, we're all bored and Miss calls the session over. All the boxes are repacked and we compare answers. Our table gets six out of ten and we're top of the class.

'Well I know you're all thinking, "What's this all about?" Well, it is about sex,' Mrs Richards declares.

Everyone cheers.

'It's about sexual attraction and the pressures you girls face to conform to impossible ideas of beauty. In most societies, women are controlled in some way from the moment they are born till they die. When society controls women, this is called what, Blue Table?'

'Marriage!' Sorayah calls out.

'Not quite.'

'Slavery!' Sorayah tries again.

'Almost.'

'A Bad Thing!' is Sorayah's third shot at it.

'It is, but that's not its name,' Mrs Richards smiles.

Jennifer steps in. 'Patriarchy, Miss.'

'Thank you Jennifer, that is correct. It exists in one form or another in all societies. Patriarchy. In some places girls are not even allowed to go to school.'

'Where's that, Miss? I wanna live there!' shouts Sorayah.

Everyone's rocking off their chair, laughing.

'It's not funny, Sorayah, it's serious,' says Mrs Richards. 'And that is only one, obvious example of how society makes women less equal than men.'

'That sucks, Miss,' says Sorayah.

'It does suck, Sorayah,' says Miss, 'on many levels. There are more subtle ways women are controlled. Think of all the insulting words used to describe women. They are often offensive words. Does anybody know any?'

'Can we say them, Miss?' says Sorayah. The whole class leans in waiting for the answer.

'Go ahead,' Miss says.

The class erupts into swear words like fireworks going off on Bonfire Night.

Everyone's jumping around, screaming out. I'm on my chair, giving it large. I drag Mikaela up on hers and we shoot off a dozen swear words. Sorayah's under her desk, killing herself with tears, even Jennifer's loosened her tie and is wagging a finger at each classmate saying bad words. Half the class are volleying the words at Mrs Richards, pointing at her as they shout. It's like a heavy metal concert, but madder, and Mrs Richards is the lead singer. I catch Mikaela's totally belly-ache laughing. She's not miserable now. I knew PSHE wouldn't let us down.

Finally Mrs Richards calls a halt. Everyone sits down again and there's silence.

'C*nt!' someone whispers.

'We've had that one,' says Miss. 'Any new words?'

'Blonde. Meaning dumb?' goes Jennifer.

'Excellent, Jennifer.'

'I'm going to tell my dad you're teaching us all men are dickheads!' Sorayah calls out.

'Tell him we're trying to change the world so his daughter has an equal chance in life,' Mrs Richards answers.

'I prefer "all men are dickheads", Miss,' insists Sorayah. Everyone agrees.

The bell goes.

'Your homework!'

Everyone groans.

'I want you to answer the question: Why are women given impossible ideals of beauty to live up to, like in the pictures? Is it our choice? Is it advertising? Is it innocent fun? Your answers should include a mention of "Patriarchy" P.A.T.R.I.A.R.C.H.Y.'

There's more groans.

Me and Mikaela join the mad scramble in the corridors and charge through the car park then out of the school grounds. The sun's blazing. There's loads of parents' cars lined up on the street as usual. We walk together towards the bus stop. I'm guessing that, because Mikaela's dad's run off, presumably with their Bentley, Mikaela will have to catch the bus home, like me. I chat and chat and chat to Mikaela so she can't even think about this.

'PSHE was well good wasn't it? How to spot fake Supermodels!'

'Yeah. What are we meant to have?' Mikaela goes. 'Tiny waists, long legs, big boobs?' She prods me, playfully. 'You've got two out of three, Adele, I've got none, it's not fair. I've got a really fat arse. Mum calls it my African bum, but I know it's fat.'

'I thought boys liked that? A Brazilian booty? Isn't it meant to be sexy?'

'Yeh. That and shaved pubes, I think. But I mean, really? Shaved pubes must be well scratchy!'

We giggle.

'Mum says boys are all a waste of time anyway. Sister, I'm telling ya, forget men, it takes a woman to make a revolution!'

I laugh and try to keep us laughing as we walk along

an endless row of parents' cars. Then I spot a Bentley and Mikaela's mum's waving to us from the driver's seat of it. 'Look!' I shout to Mikay.

Mikay leaps in the air. She gives me a quick high five then dashes to her mum.

Thinking about Mikaela (her slogans, her rhymes, her African bum, her neat passing skills, and her tears of laughter in PSHE) has me feeling good on the bus home.

Three Different Ways Mikaela Is Good To Me.

☺ SHE SAT NEXT TO ME ON DAY ONE AT SCHOOL AND HAS SAT NEXT TO ME EVER SINCE.

☺ SHE RINGS ME BACK WHEN I SILENT CALL HER BECAUSE SHE KNOWS I ONLY DO IT WHEN I DON'T HAVE CREDIT.

☺ SHE HUGS ME FOR NO REASON SOMETIMES.

I think about the PSHE lesson a bit more. Then, as I get nearer home, I start thinking about my mum.

CHAPTER 12

DOUBLE TROUBLE

It's Saturday and I get up early. The kitchen's a mess. There's a burnt out candle on the fridge and red wax all down the side. I clear it up, bin two empty bottles of vodka then go out into the garden. I'm practising twist-and-shoot when Mum hollers me. I check my watch. 11.32am. I've been training for three hours. I do my drag-the-ball-back, flick-it, bounce-it-on-my-knee-and-flick-it to-the-other-foot trick for Mum.

Mum shouts, 'I'm making you some lunch. Fish and parsley sauce!'

I give her the thumbs up, not because I'm hungry but because it's ages since she's cooked me anything.

After thirty minutes, I switch to half volley shots. The first time I try one, the ball bounces up faster than I expect. I miskick it and it balloons up. I hear it hit a kitchen window behind the shrubs.

Boosh! The window smashes.

Mum storms out. She weaves round the shrubs towards me and I can tell she's been necking vodka. She's got a plate in her hand, full of steaming food. She tries to chuck it at me. It lands on the grass about a metre away from her.

'Salmon in parsley sauce, with petals of glass! You know how long that took me? You're the devil's child! I should have had an abortion!'

'Fuck you!' I reply.

I rush inside and throw on some clothes then run back out. I can't believe what my mum has just said. It's everything I thought she ever thought of me. I wipe away enough tears so I can see the screen of my phone. Four messages from MC. I wasn't going to do this again, but I've changed my mind. I text Mikaela.

Forty minutes later, me and Mikaela are on the bus and I'm a world away from my mum.

'What's up?' Mikaela asks when she plonks herself down next to me.

I shake my head. I'm too upset to talk.

'Suit yourself.'

I don't say anything to Mikaela for a long time. We're on the back seat. Mikaela looks out of the window. The sun is blazing through Mikaela's Afro. She's lip-synching to a song on her headphones. I nudge her and she hands me an ear piece. We get a hand dance going and soon we're rocking and everyone on the bus is smiling except some old fart who starts tutting (which makes it even better).

My mum texts me.

So sorry. Can you ring me?

I text her back.

Nt now mum am w frends.

I hope she gets the friends bit. She's never been my friend.

The main square in town is full of jugglers and dancers and a big crowd's out in the sun enjoying it. MC has been here all morning and says it's pickpocket heaven. Me and Cakes know what to do. MC goes through it for Mikaela. As she explains our routine (one of us barges into someone "accidentally", the other one lifts their purse or wallet. They pass it to the third person, who takes off), I see Mikaela's cheek start its twitch. When MC has finished, I say, 'Cakes bumps, MC picks, I walk with. Watch and learn from the experts, right, MC?'

'Yup,' says MC. She does her double-jointed fingers trick for Mikaela, moving the fingers of her right hand so they revolve in strange and unnatural ways. As she does this she rolls her eyes into her head so you can only see the whites. It's MC's party trick, and just like she intended, it spooks Mikaela.

'This feels so wrong,' Mikaela whispers to me as we're walking.

MC hears her. 'The best fun always is,' she says.

'What about all the CCTV?'

'Lazy bastards what watch them are all asleep.' MC puts her hand out. Mikaela looks around nervously as we say our slogan.

'A rob for one is a rob for all!'

It isn't long before we spot someone. A woman with two toddlers pushing a buggy. Her open handbag is slung across the buggy handles. The toddlers are pulling her this way and that. We're about to crowd her when this guy in a track suit runs up with two ice creams and thrusts them at the kids. His hands go on the buggy handles and the woman scoops up her handbag and closes it. We look for someone else.

MC Banshee spots a man standing on some steps, opposite a hotel talking into his phone. She says she can see the bulge of his wallet in his inside jacket pocket. Cakes leads, pretending to be arguing with a boyfriend on her phone. At the last second she stumbles into the man, using her weight to wobble him. MC is in his jacket in a flash as he's trying to untangle himself from Cakes. MC palms me the wallet. I'm down the street as Cakes and MC are still apologising to the business guy. He swats them away while keeping up his conversation on his phone. Mikaela's with me. We run down a side street, take the stone steps down onto a canal bank and half walk, half run under a bridge. I take out the wallet. It's bulging. I unzip it. A huge bundle of notes. In three currencies. My heart is hammering my rib cage as I count them. Two hundred in English pounds. Two hundred and fifty in Euros, and ten twenty dollar USA notes. Plus four credit cards.

MC and Cakes come running up. MC's annoyed that we've opened the wallet before she caught up with us. She grabs it off us.

Ten minutes later, we're in a Fruit Slurp Bar, sipping smoothies. Mikaela is drooling over a Coconut and Mango Medley. MC grabs her in a hold that is part head lock, part friendly neck massage and says: 'So Mikaela, does it "feel so wrong" now?'

Mikaela smiles. And for the first time ever, I see a glint

of pure evil rise in her eyes. I think, *ohmygod I've created a monster.*

Cakes says we should stop robbing for the day cos we've got so much already. I agree, but MC says let's do Kendals. It's a massive department store on the rich side of the city centre and it could have been designed by shoplifters – full of lifts, stairs and escalators, eight exits, rubbish cameras and bored staff. Plus it's stuffed with the most expensive brands on earth. It has a restaurant at the top where you get a free cream cake if you have a receipt above ten pounds. We finish our smoothies and pour out into Market Street, heading for Kendals.

There's a silver statue guy in the middle of the street with a crowd around him. He's frozen on one leg in a sitting angle that means he should fall down but he doesn't. He's got a stiff scarf around his neck sticking out sideways like he's piloting an open-top airplane except we can't see the plane. People walk round him, staring. Nobody can figure out how he stays in the position he's in. There's gasps when he moves a hand to thank someone who drops money in his bowler hat on the ground. Cakes drops him a pound. He nods then freezes again.

Further up, there's a beat box kid in a back-to-front cap, four break dancers doing rubbish moves on lino and an artist copying a photo of Mona Lisa onto the pavement. After Mona Lisa we come across the white faced, statue-on-a-box-in-a-white-bed-sheet guy we saw on the bus. He's rubbish compared with the airplane guy. I giggle with Cakes. MC Banshee whispers to Mikaela, then saunters up to him. I can tell from MC's swagger she's going to do something. Mikaela's right behind her.

Me and Cakes are chewing pretzels, hanging back.

Suddenly MC rushes at him and pushes him off his box. Mikaela ducks down and scoops coins out of his money plate. They both leg it, laughing. The statue man hitches up his bed-sheet and gives chase but he trips up and goes sprawling. The crowd laughs at him. Me and Cakes walk past. Our pretzels are rammed right into the back of our mouths so we don't laugh. He's swearing in a foreign language.

Mikaela agrees to be the turnstile in Kendals. We sail up and down the escalators and stairs for a bit, to show her the ropes.

Perfume is tough in Kendals because the perfume stalls all have their own commissioned sellers watching eagle-eyed as you go past. All the women on the perfume stalls have pouty lips and botox eyebrows. Mrs Richards would be appalled. We spray a few testers on each other till they get jumpy with us, thinking we're timewasters. It's great seeing their faces when MC Banshee says, 'Do you take European money?'

Then she buys an expensive small bottle of perfume in the store with a roll of Euros. She opens the packaging there and then and starts spraying all of us with it. Suddenly the perfume sellers love us. We waltz away from their plastic, pouty smiles.

The fifth floor sells electronic goods. Cakes wants an iPod. We could buy it, but she wants to lift it.

Cakes and Mikaela go up to one end of the counter. The shop assistant takes out the tray of iPods. That's the cue for me and MC to saunter up to the other end. Cakes tries a bit of hair twirling and batting of her eyes but it doesn't distract the shop assistant. MC does a loud 'excuse me'. The shop assistant is torn. He looks over at MC then he looks back at Cakes. Cakes has already taken an iPod from the tray when he turned to look over at MC. Cakes sticks her bottom lip out and frowns like she's saying she doesn't like any of the iPods. The assistant shoves the tray back under the glass without counting the iPods, and scoots over to MC Banshee and me.

MC does good Geek and she asks lots of questions about digital radios. I look around as MC is chatting this rubbish to see if there are any store detectives following Cakes and Mikaela, who are on the move towards the stairs. If there are, I'll text them to dump the stuff in the toilets. It all looks good though, just grannies and granddads gawping at big screen TVs and a few Anoraks on Playstation consoles. I nudge MC. She makes excuses to the assistant and we take a couple of escalators down, making sure no-one's trailing us. Then we meet up with Cakes and Mikaela in Kitchenware.

Cakes looks calm. Mikaela's eyes are swishing like windscreen wipers.

'Anyone followed you?' asks MC.

They shake their heads.

'Anyone watching us now?' MC scratches her cheek as she says this, turns and picks up a frying pan. She examines it, glancing around in the pan's reflection for cameras and people.

'Who's she?' MC says, under her breath.

There's an old biddy in pearls and a fur coat, looking at sieves.

'I seen her before,' says Mikaela, 'I think she's shoplifting herself actually. She's really shifty.'

MC Banshee pauses. We glance over. Sure enough, the old biddy drops an egg timer into her pocket.

MC Banshee's eyes are screaming with laughter, but she gets it under control.

'Let's do this,' she says.

Both me and MC make to take the iPod off Mikaela. That way if they are onto us they can't be sure who has it. From a distance it just looks like three girls in a huddle, greeting one another. I've got it but MC peels away from Mikaela and takes the escalator for the Dior exit. She's doing the show run. It flushes out anybody who's been following us. We wait. Nothing happens. I examine a couple of pans. Mikaela peels off. Then Cakes. I'm on my own. Ninety seconds later, I take the stairs for the Hermes scarves exit. The iPod is snug in the back of my trouser waistband.

There's something about that moment before you go through an exit door when you're shoplifting that is the biggest thrill. You've checked the tag is off. No scruffy guys in jeans are waiting at the Exit doors. No Uniforms are lurking. Still, your senses tingle. It's the moment. You can always, at this point, back down, retrace your steps, pretend you've forgotten something and go back, dump the goods. Or you can panic and suddenly make a run for it. That might blow your cover, but if they're on to you, it might give you an edge. Decisions. You're in the zone. Maybe they've installed a new security system this day, or got some new theft alert stuff hidden in what you're robbing. A shoplifter, like a striker, has to keep her head, accept the pressure, but never forget the goal. Shoot. Score. Lift.

I'm through the detector panels and no alarm. I'm three steps away from the double Exit doors. They swing either way. Yet something's not right. It's the old lady with pearls. She's coming up fast. Why is she wearing a fur coat on a hot day? Maybe she's rich and wants to show off. She's got stubble. *Stubble*? I put a sprint on but she charges me to the floor. I kick her off me, helped by a shopping couple who think she's an old lady who's tripped over. I'm through the double doors. I glance back. Her wig's off now. Crew cut haircut. It's a man. Jeez. I step it up. I'm outside, running across the store's front. Then **bang!**

It's the white-face statue man. He holds onto me like his life depends on it. I kick at him but his white sheet tangles my legs. Now the bloke in pearls has caught up and wallops me from the side. I'm down and they're sitting on me. I wriggle but they've got me down good. I try and lose the iPod from my waistband as they drag me to my feet, but I can't reach it. The crew cut has been joined by one of his mates with a walkie-talkie. They say thanks to the statue man who is kicking me in the ribs. He spits on me. They thank him again and show they understand by miming thumping me and spitting on me, then wave him away. He spits on me one last time.

I'm allowed to my feet. They've got me tight by the arms and haul me back towards the store. I see Mikaela. She's standing on the pavement by the corner of the store, hand over her mouth. MC's right behind her, leaning on Cakes. They're all watching. Why don't they help me?

CHAPTER 13

THE DESPERADO OF DEEPEST CHEADLE

The store detectives drags me into a small room. It's got a desk, plastic chairs and no windows. They let go of my arms, push me into a chair and block the door by leaning against it. They don't say anything.

Which is kind of weird.

There's a knock. A woman comes in.

'We are detaining you because we have reasonable grounds to believe you attempted an act of theft of an iPod,' the woman says. She is burly, with blonde hair and a jaw that wobbles from side to side as she talks. She's standing above me and little drops of spit land in my face as she talks, so I look down.

'I now need to formally ask your permission to search you. If you refuse, we will detain you here until the police arrive and you will be searched anyway, possibly strip-searched. Do I have your permission to search?'

I feel along the back of my trousers, take out the iPod and hand it to her.

'One up to the old lady then!' Pearls Guy says, making a fist and shaking it to the ceiling.

'Wait till the end of the day, Playstation Kid is gonna race up the board,' says his skinnier mate. I notice now that Pearls Guy's mate does look a bit like one of the Anoraks who were playing on the consoles in Entertainment.

Pearls Guy gets on his mobile to what sounds like the police.

The woman says, 'I'm back out, then.'

'No,' they both go, 'it's a female, you have to stay on.'

'Does it matter?' the woman says. 'It's all on camera.' Her eyes tip upwards. I notice the little black dome in the top corner of the room. They don't ask me any more questions but all three of them stay in the room with me.

Playstation Kid goes, and then Pearls Guy and the woman talk about how to clip dogs' toenails and whether the Canary Islands is any good as a holiday destination. Pearls Guy leans on the door as they chat.

What-ifs and whys tumble around in my mind. What if Mikaela hadn't missed Pearls Guy when she was turnstiling? What if MC and Mikaela hadn't wound up Statue Man? (How did Statue Man even get there?) Why did he grab me when he didn't before? What if all three of them, instead of watching as I got flattened outside the store, had actually helped me?

There's a knock on the door. A policeman in uniform comes in.

'Only one then?' he says, looking disappointed.

'It's all on camera,' Pearls Guy replies. 'We'll bung you a tape.'

I'm numb when the cop pulls me up off my seat. I'm led through the Perfume concessions, which has the Pouty

Ladies all tutting, through the front exit doors into the crowds and along the side of Kendals to a police van.

This is all a mistake, I say to myself to keep cool, *it's a scene we're shooting for a Hollywood movie, I'm not a thief, I'm a film star.*

The cop swings the van doors open. He pushes me up and in. Two sets of metal doors slam shut behind me. The van smells of flowers and sick.

It isn't long before we stop and I'm in a procession stepping out of the van into the grounds of some high-walled police station courtyard. I'm numb. I hadn't noticed anyone else get inside the van. I'm led, fourth in line, to a Reception. For a moment I think about giving a false name and address, but it seems pointless so I give them what they ask for. They take my possessions which I have to sign a form about. The policeman behind the big Reception desk gives me a friendly smile, which is weird. He says lots of things to me that I don't listen to. Then he says:

'Welcome to Bootle Street Hotel. Don't look so worried, you'll be out soon. We're not putting you in cells as it is my judgement you are a minor and pose no risk to yourself or others.'

I feel myself wanting to wee.

I'm led down a corridor and into a room where there's lots of other people at desks though no-one's in uniform. I'm shown to a seat in front of a desk with a telephone and computer on it and I sit there wondering what next. The room is hot. Eventually a man comes and slides behind the desk.

'Adele,' he says, 'You were caught red handed with let's

see ... an iPod. You don't deny that, do you?'

I shrug.

'I'll make this as painless as possible for you,' he continues. 'We've checked the databases and you have no other arrests to your name, nothing. It might not be the first time you've done this, but it's the first time you've been caught. Am I right?'

I say nothing again. His tie has some kind of ketchup stain on it. His desk phone starts ringing.

'If it is your first time, here's how it works. We won't seek prosecution. The store will allow that, it's the understanding we have with them, but only if you admit what you did.'

The phone stops.

'Can I go now then?' I ask.

'No you can't,' he says.

'Why not?'

'We can't just release you. You're a minor.' He sighs. 'We have a major terrorist alert on and here I am wasting time with you.'

The phone starts again.

'OK, what we need to do now is phone Mum or Dad to come and collect you.'

He's got my phone already. I watch him scrolling through till he finds what he's looking for. He gets there.

'Who's it to be then, Mum or Dad?'

I shrug. I can't tell whether he's trying to be nice or teasing me. He has wonky teeth. He dials a number. There's no answer and it cuts out quickly. That's Mum's phone, she's always switched off. He rings another number. It rings for an eternity. Dad doesn't like answerphone messages. He

94

says too many people can hack into them.

The policeman scratches his nose. He knows they're the right numbers because I haven't had the chance to mess with my phone.

'Why don't they pick up?' he asks.

'Probably switched off.'

'Mmm. We can drive you home. Unless you know of another responsible adult who might pick you up? Help us out, we're a bit busy here, Adele.'

'My boyfriend's mum,' I say.

He grimaces. 'We need your parents or someone acting as a parent – a guardian. It has to be a responsible adult, else we have to drive you home ourselves, or find a Youth Justice worker. On a Saturday.'

As he says that, someone calls out in the office and asks, 'Dave, you wrapped that up yet?'

'Ring her and see,' I say.

He walks away to the far corner of the office and phones Marcus's mum. It's a long call. His face shifts from frowning, to puzzled, to amused, then loops all the way back to frowning again. Eventually, he comes back to the desk and nods. 'She's acceptable,' is all he says.

Eight minutes later Mrs Adenuga is in the police station office and rushing up to me. 'Adele! What have you got yourself into?'

I fling my arms around her, take a few deep breaths and let the only tear I shed in that police station escape. 'I'm sorry, Mrs Adenuga,' I mumble. It's all I can manage.

'Shh. There, there.'

The policeman butts in. He's restless. 'Now, you don't

deny you stole the iPod?'

'I took it out of the shop,' I say. What I am not saying is that I lifted it. I didn't. That was Cakes.

'We can look at the footage,' he says.

'OK, I took it,' I say. *What difference does it make?*

He's happy now. He clicks his mouse a few times, then looks up again. 'Adele, because it's a first offence and you admit that you did it, I'm allowed to issue you with a youth caution. That means we keep a record and if you are ever caught shoplifting again, we can charge you. Be advised.'

As he is talking, he's typing. A printer whirrs somewhere under his desk.

He ducks down and scoops up some paper. It's got the police logo on it at the top.

'Sign here,' he says. 'And here.'

As I'm signing, he reads from his computer screen. 'You may get an Acceptable Behaviour Contract and a Youth Engagement Officer may check up on how you're doing. You are now banned from Kendals. Understand?'

I nod.

The cop has Mrs Adenuga sign a piece of paper. As she signs, she says, 'David isn't it? Are you happy with the windows here, David? Why aren't they open? It's tropical in this office.'

'They're all jammed. Half of them rotten as well,' he replies.

She gives him a card. 'Get this to the right person. Ask them to give me a call. You'll get a great price. None of you need to be sweating in here any longer.'

The policeman laughs. They chat for a bit more, then

96

he looks over to me. 'Adele, we don't want to see you again, understood?'

I nod. I think he actually means it.

'Thank you, Officer, it's much appreciated,' says Mrs Adenuga. 'I'm so sorry about my niece.'

I catch her eyes. She looks back at me like, *don't say a word*.

The cop weaves us through various other offices back to Reception where we sign out and they hand me the rest of my stuff back.

On the open street, breathing free air once more, tears spill out of me. I feel Mrs Adenuga stroking my face.

'I'm so ashamed,' I say to her. Mrs Adenuga leads me the rest of the way to the car. It has a parking ticket on the windscreen. She sees it and makes sucking noises. Marcus is in the front passenger seat. My heart flips.

Marcus makes to get out of the car but his mum is already pushing me into the rear. She rips the parking ticket off the window, stabs the key in the ignition and the car lurches off. Marcus sneaks a hand back towards me. I take it and for a minute there's silence in the car as me and Marcus hold hands and his mum drives. The parking ticket plastic wrapper flutters on the dashboard.

'I promised that nice policeman I'd drop you home into the custody of your parents,' Mrs Adenuga says, finally breaking the spell, 'what's the address?'

She stabs my post code and house number into the car's satnav while she's driving and drives through two traffic lights on yellow. I take my cue from Marcus and say nothing all the way. We arrive at my house.

I hold my breath. If it's Mum and she's not drugged up, there'll be wailing, tears as a show for Mrs Adenuga, then she'll build herself a huge spliff and forget about it. If it's Dad, he'll probably rant then drive off.

Mrs Adenuga gets out of the car and rings the buzzer by the gates. She's ringing and ringing. Nobody's in. I try ringing the house from my phone. Nobody picks up. Mrs Adenuga gets back in the car and hesitates.

'You really live here?' she asks me. She's impressed by the size of it.

'The top left one is my room,' I say, pointing.

'How are your windows?'

'Mum!' groans Marcus.

'They're fine,' I say.

'I can't leave you here on your own. I'm not driving you back to the police station. You'll have to stop at ours until your mum or dad get back.'

'That's fine,' I say. I've never been inside Marcus's house before, though I've sneaked him in mine once.

Mrs Adenuga drives us off. I feel the sweat drying up in my armpit. Marcus has my hand again. We're soon on an estate of small houses with no space between them. There's a park in the middle with one set of slanting goalposts and a pack of roaming dogs. A man is playing golf there and seems to be aiming his golf balls at the dogs. Mrs Adenuga pulls up at a house facing the park and nudges the car onto the short drive.

We go in. There's a sound like a cat has got its tail stuck in a food blender but neither Marcus nor his mum look concerned. Mrs Adenuga pushes open the living room

98

door. A man is sitting in a swivel chair at a desk in a corner. He's got headphones on and is swaying to some music while making the cat sound.

'I just sprung your son's girlfriend out of the nick!' Mrs Adenuga calls out to him.

He half turns, gives her the thumbs-up, nods to Marcus, then me, then turns back, still wailing.

She might as well have told him she had just come back from the supermarket. It's cool with me.

'How's Leah?' she asks him, holding a remote that I assume she's pressed to cut off the sound to his headphones.

Marcus's dad swivels fully. He shows off a baby, asleep in his lap. 'New nappy, new bottle, what's not to like?' he says, then he taps his headphones. Mrs Adenuga blips the remote again and the wailing restarts.

'What he puts poor Leah through,' Mrs Adenuga mutters. She tells us to come into the kitchen. Marcus says he is starving but I'm not hungry. Mrs Adenuga makes a baked beans and ham omelette. She gives us half each. Marcus nods for me to follow him with my plate.

'Where are you going?' his mum calls out to his back.

'Mars,' he answers without missing a beat. His mum does a dramatic sigh. Marcus ignores it or doesn't hear it. He steers me through the living room and upstairs. On the landing we turn left into a room. He flicks a switch. It's his bedroom. We sit on the bed, eating. His room is nice. It has that boy smell. Lots of bar-bells and weights on the floor. Pictures of hip hop stars on the walls. A roll-on deodorant is on the floor next to a heap of clothes. School books next to the clothes. The floor is his shelving. Only when he's finished eating his half of the omelette and then mine does he ask a question, except it's not really a question.

'Not hungry?'

I shrug.

He shuffles up next to me on the edge of his bed and puts an arm round me. Which is nice.

'What was you robbing?' he asks, curious.

'Leave it,' I say. 'I'm tired.'

'Here,' he says. He turns his face into mine and kisses me. I kiss him back, a little. Then one of his hands starts roving.

I trap it under mine. 'Marcus, don't bother.'

He shrugs, but there's still mischief in his eyes. I realise I'm in his bedroom, on his bed, and he's probably got ideas. I fish out my phone and try the house line again. My brother picks up.

'Oh, it's you,' my brother says, disappointed. 'What do you want?'

'Is Mum or Dad in?' I ask.

'Both,' he says. He puts the phone down before I can say another word.

Meanwhile, Marcus is leaning in for another kiss.

I go downstairs and Marcus's mum phones me a taxi. 'Are you alright, darling?' she says.

That has me crying again. Mrs Adenuga holds me in her arms. 'We've been a very silly girl today, haven't we?' she sighs.

I nod and sniffle. 'I let you down.'

'You let yourself down,' she says.

Marcus has turned on the TV and he flicks to the football results.

Twenty minutes later I'm back at home. Neither Mum nor Dad ask any questions. *They can't know*, I decide. I make it to my room, lock the door and lie back on my bed. I'm trembling. I don't want to think about what's going to happen next.

I check my phone. MC has texted me:

Did u grass us up?

Course nt

Thnx. My cuz says thnx too

Finally there's something I can feel proud of. Adele Vialli did not snitch. And for that, all three of them owe me. Especially Mikaela. Suddenly I resent her. Nothing ever went wrong until she joined us. I remember her face when she saw me caught. Horror. Yet she hasn't contacted me since, not even a text. She's probably hiding under her bed, deleting my number from her phone so she can say she doesn't even know me. She should have rung. A true friend would have rung.

I'm a criminal now, I realise. I've been nicked. I imagine a poster like the Wild West ones with my face on it.

WANTED FOR LARCENY.
ADELE VIALLI,

VILLAIN AT LARGE
HIDE YOUR VALUABLES.
LOCK YOUR DOORS.
THE DESPERADO FROM
DEEPEST CHEADLE IS RUNNING
AMOK IN YOUR AREA.

CHAPTER 14

QUESTIONS, QUESTIONS.

My alarm clock says Sunday, 8.21 am. The house is asleep. MTB spent Saturday evening at the gym inflating his biceps and is probably recuperating. Mum's snoozing after a late night binge. Dad was out all night entertaining Iraqi Government Bankers. What entertainment does he lay on, I wonder, as I paint my big toe nails pink. His impressions of Italian-American film stars take up all of two minutes. What's after that? Maypole dancing? The hokey cokey? Pass The Parcel?

I check on Mum to make sure she hasn't vomited or anything. She's curled up and snoring. Dad's sleeping with her. He's stretched out like a high board diver before they plunge. He's got a death look on his face. I pull a bit of the duvet off Dad and over to Mum because Mum's got no quilt at all. Then I tiptoe out.

Bacon can wake the dead so I boil eggs first. Within two minutes of bacon hitting the frying pan MTB comes down. He's grumpy, smelly and bed-headed. He's followed by Dad who's like a dozy bear, all scratching and farting and puzzled, like he's not sure he's in the right house. Then comes Mum who flicks her tongue out like a lizard tasting air and scratches herself in all areas. Mum and Dad have both got this vacant look in their eyes and don't give each other any eye contact, so they may even have been at it this morning. All in all, it's not a scene that helps keep your breakfast in your stomach, so I flip all the bacon onto one huge plate, then leave them to their scratchy, smelly, tongue-flicking, smutty selves.

I'm back in my bedroom painting my toenails green this time to see how they'd look, when Dad shouts me to come downstairs. I go down. He's in his PJs still, and he's got his phone in his hand. Mum's leaning against the fridge. MTB is smirking into his cornflakes. There's two rashers of bacon left.

'Adele,' calls Dad, in his annoyed voice, 'I've just had the most bizarre phone call. From the police. Allegedly. Have you been setting up prank calls again? Adele? Did you set this up?

'It is *not* a prank call!' Mum grumbles at him.

'How do you know?' Dad says. 'One pound fifty for the pleasure of winding up your parents. You know our Adele.'

'Are you sure it's the police? Maybe it's the private detective I'm paying to follow you. The Infidelity Expert.'

'Adele?' says Dad, ignoring Mum.

'Yes?' I reply. ("Adele?" is not actually a full question, so I don't say any more.)

'They're telling me you were apprehended for shoplifting. Is that true?'

There's a pause. Everyone's leaning in.

'What does "apprehended" mean?' I ask.

MTB's smirk takes over his entire face.

'Caught. Adele?'

'Yes, it's true,' I blurt.

'You stupid, stupid girl!' shouts Dad. He kicks a chair. 'Shoplifting? Really? I mean why? There's no percentage in it. Rob a bank I can understand. But a shop? Give me strength!'

'I've got to start somewhere,' I snap back, 'before I get to your bank-robbing level!'

But Dad doesn't hear a word, he's still in his rant. 'Shoplifting? Of all things. Just plain stupid!'

'Ohmygod!' says Mum, arm-fainting onto the fridge door. 'Someone's taken my vodka again!'

'Can you shut up about your vodka for just one day in the week?'

Dad chucks his phone at a kitchen wall. It breaks into the usual pieces. MTB sneaks another piece of bacon.

Dad turns, calmer (chucking things always calms him). He looks puzzled. 'Have you not got enough things? Don't we give you...?'

Mum's clinging to Dad's throwing arm and is pressing him down into a kitchen chair. Dad looks lost and I'm not sure what he's going to do next. He could cry, dance or rant again.

MTB cackles.

'Anthony, go to your room!' Mum says.

'Why?' he complains.

'Because,' says Mum.

'Am I the criminal here?' he moans. 'Am I the one robbing shops or banks? Why am I the one who has to get locked in his room?'

'Nobody's locking you in your room,' Mum says. 'Just go upstairs for a while. Your father and I need to have a conversation with your sister.'

Mum's icy politeness is well scary. I've never heard her more sober.

Mouthing swear words, MTB swipes the last bacon rasher and leaves the room.

I sit down, spread my fingers across my face and wait. 'I'm sorry,' I say. 'It was a bit of fooling around that got out of hand.'

'This is all your fault,' Dad says to Mum. 'If you paid her more attention...'

'She's a Daddy's Girl,' says Mum, 'and she's only doing what you do for a living, but on a smaller scale.'

'Can you please stop grinding away about that? I am not like all bankers.'

'It's the only grinding I get to do nowadays,' mutters Mum.

'I thought this was about me?' I say to them both.

'What?' they both turn and say.

I realise I'm not needed, I'm just an excuse for them to argue again really. I bury my head in my hands. I'm not crying. I'm just tired.

'What was it you were stealing?' Mum asks.

Robbing is not about what you lift, it's about running with friends and the thrill. But what's the point of explaining? I think.

'Jewellery,' I reply to Mum.

'Jewellery?' she says, like it's some astonishing new invention that she has to get her head around. 'Don't you have jewellery already?'

'Fashionable jewellery.'

'What is fashionable jewellery?'

'You know, brand names.'

At the pace Mum's questions are going, this could take weeks. I'm still sitting at the table.

'Don't you have brand name jewellery already?'

I've nicked loads, but Mum doesn't know that.

'No,' I say.

'Umm,' says Mum, 'You're becoming a woman. Every woman likes jewellery, preferably as a gift from her partner to show her he loves her.'

Dad ignores this dig and says, 'The police said it was an iPod, not jewellery. Unless you took jewellery as well and they don't know?'

MTB has tiptoed down again and is lurking in the door frame, making prat faces at me.

'Well, did you?' says Mum, curious.

'No. Dad's right.'

'Then why are we talking about jewellery?' Mum sighs.

They've got it all tangled up now, but I can't be bothered.

'iPods are like jewellery,' I say.

'I need a drink,' Mum says as she walks out.

'This isn't good,' concludes Dad.

No shit, Sherlock, I reply to Dad in my head.

'This could have repercussions,' he continues.

I imagine Sherlock Holmes passing Dad his pipe and saying, "Puff away, Mr Vincent Vialli, you're far sharper than me: hats off to you."

'They said they might send a support worker or something around.'

Mum does a little yelp from inside the garage where she's gone to look for her drinks stash.

'If they can find one,' Dad continues. 'This could stop you playing for England. The sponsorship deal would be off.'

'What sponsorship deal?' I ask.

'Never mind,' says Dad. He shakes his head a bit then repeats, 'You stupid, stupid girl.'

Mum comes back with a full bottle of vodka. 'Stop hiding my things!' she says to me with venom. 'I know it's you!'

She pours some vodka into a glass and takes a gulp, then necks the whole glass and refills it in one smooth action. *Even if I don't get to play for England, Mum could drink for England*, I think to myself.

Dad looks at me and we both know. Third glass and she'll lose it.

Sure enough she throws back the third glass and she's wailing. She flings herself into Dad's arms. Dad peels her off. She staggers over and falls on me. She's hugging me from behind, around the neck. One of those hugs that might easily slip into a bit of strangling. She strokes my hair. 'Oh, Adele,' she says, 'Oh, my baby.'

I know she's feeling sorry for herself, not me. Nevertheless, I burst into tears. Mum bursts into more tears. Dad shakes his head and chokes a sob. It's a tear fest. MTB rolls his eyes and ducks away from the doorway. I hear his footsteps up the stairs.

I let Mum stroke my hair a little longer then I untangle myself from her and get up from the chair. 'Is it OK if I go to my room, now, Mum?' I ask.

'Yes,' she snaps. She stares at Dad. He's picking up the pieces of his phone. 'But don't steal anything on your way up!'

When I reach my room I catch my brother rifling through my undies drawer. 'Get out of there, idiot, that's where I keep my tampons!' I rush over. He turns before I reach him and in his hand he's clutching the bracelets. He holds them high above his head. I beat him on the chest but he's built like a horse and it has no effect, so I kick him in the nuts. He buckles and drops the bracelets.

'What did. You do. That. For?' he gasps.

'It was a favour,' I say. 'You should know not to mess with my things. I've told you before, big brother.'

'How is. This a. Favour?'

'These are hot property.' I gather the bracelets up. 'Get your fingerprints on them and the police might lock *you* up.'

'Get rid of them then,' MTB says. Cursing me softly, he limps off to nurse his assets in cold water.

I can hear Mum and Dad arguing downstairs still. Something crashes against a wall. Mum doesn't scream though, so I don't go down. MTB puts 50 Cents on loop, at max. I dance along a bit with all my bracelets on. I check the mirror. I look mega-blinged, though my PJs look crusty. I hide the bracelets in a bra cup in my laundry basket. The laundry doesn't get done much since Mia left and MTB won't think to go rummaging in there. I find a towel from my wardrobe, pluck my football boots out of my boots bucket and wipe the rest of the mud off them with the towel.

Mum is shouting at MTB to 'take that off'. 50 Cents is replaced by that Xmas song, "Walking In The Air" (MTB's idea of a joke). She yells at him to turn that down too because it's doing her head in. I hear Dad's car spray gravel outside, so I know Dad's done a runner. That's going to make Mum even more miserable. Later, she will go and sit with MTB in his room for a while and have him talk about whether he will become a doctor, a lawyer or a professional footballer ('or maybe all three!' Add giggles here from both MTB and Mum). Then she'll test him on his homework and they'll end up downstairs on the sofa together watching some Musical. My brother plays Mum so well. He presses all her buttons just the way she likes, then at the right moment he taps her for twenty pounds to buy protein shakes and waltzes off to meet up with his gym buddies.

I find my phone and glance at it. There's nothing from Mikaela. But Marcus has texted me.

Bored. Can u come round?

Can birds fly? I tell Mum I'm off to do my homework at a friend's house. She's in MTB's room, absorbed by his yawn-inducing story about a wasp in his classroom (a story which is probably untrue since he skips school so much). She gives me the taxi fare and smiles me away. Not long after I'm outside Marcus's house .

Marcus opens the door and I follow him into the lounge. The smell of dirty nappy hits my nose. Steam is billowing in from the kitchen. Some reggae track is playing. Marcus's dad is rolling around on the floor with little Leah. Leah's face is all glee. The TV is on in the background. Marcus's mum is at the coffee table with three identical steel tumblers, talking to herself while trying some magic trick.

She waves me over. 'Take a seat, Adele, darling.'

The only empty seats are either side of her on the sofa. I sit to her left. She says to Marcus:

'One more time, sweetie.'

Marcus is standing in front of her. 'Mum, you're hopeless,' he says, 'Give up.'

'I'll get you this time,' says his mum.

Marcus does a big, lip vibrating sigh and says, 'No chance.' He squats in front of the coffee table. His mum shows him a dice then starts shuffling the tumblers quickly, so fast I can't track which tumbler the dice is under. As she does this she's chanting, 'left, right left, left-left, right'. She stops.

'Which one?' she calls out to him.

Marcus taps a tumbler. The left.

His mum lifts it. The dice is there.

'Lucky sod,' she says, 'Again!'

Marcus does his dimple grin, runs his hand through his hair and shrugs. His mum lines up the tumblers again. She redoes her routine.

'Choose!'

He taps middle this time. He's right again. Marcus chooses right four times in a row but his mum won't let up. The soup smell has got an under-sniff of burn to it now.

I twitch my nose. 'Is something burning? I ask innocently.

'Oh, sheez,' says his mum, and scrambles off the sofa.

I check my phone. Mikaela hasn't rung in all this time.

Marcus plonks himself down next to me as his dad clears the coffee table, parks a baby mat on it and starts changing Leah's nappy.

'You shouldn't of let my mum off the hook,' Marcus says, digging me in the ribs. 'I can always spot the dice, she's too slow.'

I chuckle. 'Something *was* burning.'

'She likes you,' his dad says of Leah, who has wrapped four little fingers around one of mine.

She's adorable. I try some baby talk. 'Googoo, gaagaa.'

'Brumusshh,' replies Leah, gurgling.

Marcus groans.

'You the girlfriend then?' his dad says to me.

'I'm helping her with her maths homework,' Marcus says, quickly.

'Righty-o,' says his dad, with a wink at me.

'Who wants stew?' Mrs Adenuga calls out.

'Do you want some help?' I ask her.

She nods and we go into the kitchen. As I'm helping find plates, Leah has crawled in and wrapped herself between my legs. Mrs Adenuga corners me. 'I hope that episode was a one-off, young lady,' she says.

I nod. I want to hide in the washing machine.

'I can't have my son corrupted,' she adds. 'He's got prospects. He might even make it to university.'

She makes university sound like reaching the top of Mount Everest.

'I'm sorry,' I say, 'I won't do it again.'

'But why, Adele? I'm not being funny but your family is loaded. You're not shoplifting for nappies like most of them

112

round here.'

Suddenly, I'm crying again.

'Don't cry, love. What's done is done.'

She scoops Leah out of the vegetables in the bottom of the fridge where she's crawled in, closes the fridge door with her bum and puts her in my arms while she rounds up the rest of the plates. Leah glides a finger through my tears, fascinated. Then she makes a sad face, copying mine. She looks so unbelievably sad. I smile my biggest smile. Leah smiles too. I wipe my face, because I don't want Marcus seeing me like this. Leah wipes hers.

'She's smitten,' says Mrs Adenuga, as she bustles around the tiny kitchen. 'She really likes you.'

We're soon sat at the table, eating mutton stew. More accurately, Marcus's dad is chomping mutton stew; his mum is dipping her spoon into mutton stew while having an animated conversation on the phone about a Caravan Windows Conference; Marcus is pouring stew directly into his face from his plate, and Leah is trying to flick stew puree at me with a tiny plastic spoon. Occasionally, she allows me to take the spoon from her and stick it in her mouth, loaded with stew.

'What is mutton?' I ask.

'I dunno,' belches Marcus. 'Dad, what's mutton?'

'Mutton is goat,' his dad replies. 'Don't be rude, Marcus, just because you've got a guest.'

'Sheep,' his mum corrects his dad, even though she's still on the phone.

'What we are eating is goat,' his dad says emphatically to Marcus, but really to his wife. 'And this goat has been

113

inaccurately named mutton by your mother.'

'I cooked it, I should know. It's mutton,' his mum holds firm. 'Sheep.'

'OK, you're right. Mutton argue!' his dad says, in the tone of "mustn't argue". This has him and Marcus killing themselves laughing. His mum fails to see the joke.

Later, after Marcus has tried and given up teaching me the rules of quadratic equations, he drags me into the kitchen to help with his washing-up duty.

'How's it going at home, after, you know . . . what happened?' he asks me.

'How do you think it's going?' I reply.

'So they know?'

'What do you think?'

'Hey, I'm on your side.'

'Just drop it, OK? Pass a plate.'

He passes a plate. 'But why, Adele?' he says, like it's a maths problem he has to solve.

I've had enough. 'Why! Why! Why! Everyone keeps asking me why. Because. That's why!'

We finish doing the dishes in silence. His dad comes in and says, 'Like a proper married couple you two are!' He takes a beer from the fridge and goes back into the living room.

I leave shortly after. Mikaela does not pick up when I ring her from my taxi home. I manage to avoid everyone in the house. I go to bed with a headache.

CHAPTER 15

AUNTIE ASTONISHED, LIES & LETTERS

It's Monday morning, I've got the biggest headache ever, and I'm late. Dad drives me to school in silence. He hasn't shaved and he doesn't even have his work tie on. He doesn't look at me throughout the whole journey.

Monday morning assemblies are painful experiences. Rows of unwilling learners are lined up by jaded teachers to be bored to death by dull speakers. Usually, as a special treat, at the end of the assembly, a particularly ungifted and untalented member of the Gifted And Talented Club will play out of tune on an oboe or similar. If I could sell ear plugs for the event I'd have been Britain's first fourteen year old millionaire by now. Mikaela has filed in before me. I try to catch her eye but she's ignoring me so I ignore her back.

The new Head takes to the stage. I think she's Asian. She's in a grey suit and speaks twenty-two carat English. It seems she astonishes easily:

'I'm astonished,' she trills, 'that you have come into this Assembly Hall so quietly. Thank you, each of you. I am also astonished at the attendance records I have been shown. You have all made such a big effort to get to school on time and not take days off needlessly. Ninety-six percent. Well done. Give yourselves a round of applause.'

We applaud ourselves with the lack of enthusiasm only Mondays can deliver. The new Head gets through a few other things she's astonished about, before she starts to "note" things, then she's "puzzled" by things. I'm back to listening when she makes it to being "seriously concerned" with things.

'I have been reliably informed,' she intones, 'by the police no less, that there is a Criminal Gang operating from this school, stealing things from city centre shops. A Criminal Gang!'

I look across. Mikaela is six shoulders along from me. She's stopped breathing.

'I'm seriously concerned. Why any girl would consider it a good idea to do such a thing is beyond me. You have your whole future ahead of you. You are brimful of promise. Don't sacrifice that. Thieves always get caught in the end. Always.'

Auntie Astonished takes a breath then continues. 'I'm sorry to have to speak like this to the ninety nine point five percent of you who have done nothing wrong. Most of you have been exemplary. I'm astonished at your good behaviour and achievements in general.'

I'm guessing Auntie Astonished taught Maths before she became a Head teacher.

'On a more pleasant note, we are fortunate to have ....' She reads from a card. 'Jessica Barker, no, Jemima Barker, no, Gemma Barker. Is she here?'

There is a kerfuffle up front and the Chosen One emerges.

'Yes, Gemma Barker from our Gifted and Talented Club is going to play a short piece on her clarinet. Big hand for Gemma!'

After a limp applause, Gemma duly massacres something Mozart allegedly composed.

I go into English and find Mikaela has a New Best Friend and is not sitting at our desk. Instead some other girl is there and Mikaela is sitting with her New Best Friend at the next desk along. It's the first time we've ever sat apart in English. Everyone in class is feeling the vibes. I decide I'm not even talking to her. The lesson gets going. It's how to write haiku.

Mikaela whispers across at me in four syllables. 'Are you OK?'

I don't answer. If I did it would be in eight syllables: 'Stupid question. What do you care?'

Her hair is in braids again, with blonde streaks this time. She's swishing her head this way and that, making sure everyone notices. How could somebody grow enormous blonde streaks of hair over a weekend? Not possible. Duh. Like everything else about her, it's fake.

English drones on. Miss is doing the register. I answer to my name.

Mikaela leans over. 'So you haven't lost your voice after all?'

'I've got nothing to say to you,' I whisper back across the desks.

'It wasn't my fault.'

I blank her.

'What was I supposed to do?' she moans.

'Er, like maybe you could of got the Statue guy off me

before they had me pinned to the floor like a squashed rat?'

'But...' she whines.

Half the class has tuned in. People are sneaking looks at us over their shoulders. I don't care.

'That's what I would of done. But you didn't lift a finger, did you? 'Cos you're a coward!'

Mikaela's crying now, quietly. Her New Best Friend gives me the evils. I'm not bothered. Mikaela wasn't the one dumped in a police van with hard-core criminals. She wasn't the one cautioned. What does she have to cry about?

'Why did you have to rob the statue guy in the first place anyway?' I say. 'It was stupid. You silly, sad bitch!'

The New Best Friend looks at me with a face like a slapped baby's. 'Did you just call her a silly black bitch?' she exclaims. She turns to Mikaela. 'Did you hear that, Mikaela? She called you a silly black bitch!'

Mikaela kicks back her chair and comes flying across her own desk and mine. She gets me in a headlock and starts punching and scratching. I wriggle free and grab her waist and start shaking her. She screams for mercy, even though I'm not really hurting her.

Then the teacher is pulling us apart. 'You two, what's got into you? Mikaela! Look at Adele's face, Mikaela!'

'Adele called her a silly black bitch!' her New Best Friend says.

There's uproar in the classroom after that. Everyone's arguing.

'That's a lie,' I protest.

Miss doesn't want to hear it. 'Adele Vialli you are in big trouble!'

She sends someone next door and they return with two Year 11 prefects. 'Right,' Miss says, 'both of you, to Isolation!'

The prefects march us to Isolation.

I can't believe Mikaela told such a whopper. Stupid yes. Bitch yes. But black bitch? I never said it.

As we walk the corridors, Mikaela is sobbing and gasping. Both prefects have their arm around her and shoot ugly glances at me. I realise it would be better for me if I cried too, but I can't be bothered. I'm not such a faker.

It's Mrs Duras again, looking exasperated. She puts the phone down after a couple of "I see, I see"s.

'Thank you,' she says to the prefects, 'and bring me the First Aid kit before you return to your class.' She looks at us. 'Mikaela, take that seat there. Adele, over there,' she says, pointing to another chair. 'Adele, I would never in a month of Sundays have expected you to be using words like that.'

'I didn't say them, Miss. Did I say them, Mikaela? Did I?'

Mikaela doesn't answer, she just keeps up her sniffle act.

'Racism is not good, Adele. All over the world people of many backgrounds are living together, learning together. Bangladeshis in Hong Kong, Sudanese in Saudi Arabia, Mexicans in America, Africans in Europe. Racism has no future, and it will not be tolerated in this school.'

Mikaela gloats in between crocodile sniffles.

'But...' I say.

'There's no "buts". We will be taking statements from your classmates. This will go up to the new Head teacher and she will deal with it. I'm puzzled. You've been best friends for so long.'

'Tell her, Mikaela,' I say. 'I didn't say it.'

Mikaela hides her face in her sleeve. At that precise moment, I hate Mikaela with every cell of my body, even my dead skin cells hate her.

One of the prefects returns with a First Aid box. Mrs Duras dismisses her, then hands me a wet wipe from the box.

'What about me?' I say, 'what about this?' I've pressed the wet wipe against my forehead and it's already red all over with blood.

'It will heal,' Mrs Duras says, 'it's a tiny cut.'

The bell goes.

'Mikaela. Apologise for scratching her face.'

'Sorry,' says Mikaela, with a curled lip.

'Mikaela, you can go. Adele, stay here.'

Mikaela sniffles and gloats as she leaves.

It's just me and Mrs Duras. I can see there's no getting through to her so I give up trying.

'Adele, wait here while I talk to the Head. Your parents will learn of this.' Miss Duras heads off.

Between being called a racist and the shoplifting, I guess I'm well and truly stuffed at this school. The England team chance is over for me as well, I'm sure. I expect I'll be expelled. Where do people go when they're expelled? *It was an OK school*, I think, *apart from the lessons*. The uniform was not all that and the food was iffy, but the rest was OK. I'm not sure I'll bother with another school after this one. Too much hassle.

Mrs Duras is back, acid-faced. She tells me to follow her and leads me to the Head's office. It's weird going past classrooms for the last time. The chatter of the eager Year 7s. The beavering silence of the Year 8s. The sweaty Year 10's. The imperious Year 11s. Most of all, I'll miss us, the Year 9s. I'll miss Clingfilm, the geography teacher, Miss Dolphin's Art class and PSHE with Mrs Richards. If I had a hanky I'd dab my eyes. I make do with wiping my nose on my blazer sleeve.

We arrive. Mrs Duras knocks on the Head's door. The Head has had an entry system installed outside her office, like at a doctor's. Engaged is Red. Enter is Green. It's currently on Red. The light flips to Green, a buzzer sounds, and I hear her call, 'Enter!'

Mrs Duras opens the door, shoves me forward and disappears.

'You wanted to see me, Miss?' I ask, as sweetly as I can manage.

'Yes, Adele. Take a seat.'

The number of times I've been asked to take a seat recently, I could fill an arena with them, I think.

'Do you know why you're here?'

'Yes,' I say. Actually, I'm not sure. My crime sheet is so long it could be any of a number of things.

'It's a very serious matter.'

I nod. I've decided I'm going to be expelled so there is no point in fighting her, or even listening. I look around. The new Head has changed the office a bit. The filing cabinet's gone. An iPad sits on an almost empty desk with some fresh pink carnations in a small vase to one side. There's a framed photo on the other corner, but turned towards her so I can't see who's in it.

When I next tune in, Auntie Astonished is well into her stride.

'... quite frankly I am appalled by this behaviour. Poor Mikaela. Can you even imagine the hurt that you have caused her? You might have scarred her for life. How will she ever form relationships later in life with this kind of example from someone who is meant to be her best friend?'

She pauses. I smile to myself at how wrong adults can get things.

'Take that smile off your face!'

I straighten my face.

The Head piles it on. 'I've looked at Mikaela's Achievement Reports. She is exactly the kind of girl we encourage at our school. She started with very average grades. Yet she has by hard work and persistence, climbed up the Achievement Tables and is now in the top fifteen percentile for her age. I'm astonished you should try to diminish her self-esteem in this way, it's inexcusable. She is an exemplary pupil. A golden girl.'

I can't listen to any more. 'She's the one who went shoplifting with me!' I blurt out. 'She's a thief! She goes robbing with me! How golden is that? And I didn't say those frigging words!'

The Head stops playing with her iPad graphs at last. She looks at me as if I'm a specimen on the end of some microscope. A light goes on in her mind. Then promptly off again.

'That's nonsense,' she says, finally. 'Don't make up lies, Adele, you'll only dig yourself in deeper.'

I'm not bothered now. 'Wait till the police get the shop

video,' I tell her. 'Then you'll see how golden Mikaela Robinson is.'

'Are you serious, Adele? Or is this a ploy to distract attention from your potty mouth? It's a very important allegation you are making.'

'Please yourself,' I say. Mikaela is obviously some kind of patron saint in Auntie Astonished's world.

The iPad graphs blink back up. Auntie Astonished shakes her head. 'Smoke and mirrors, Adele. I will investigate, but you don't fool me. You will write a letter of apology to Mikaela, and it must be contrite.'

'What does "contrite" mean?'

Auntie Astonished exhales. 'Apologetic. And it must say you will never ever use such language again in school. You must bring me the letter. Do you understand? 'Til then you will remain in Isolation.'

'You want me to write a letter apologising for something I didn't say?'

'Don't get cute, Adele.'

'But that's so unfair!'

'Think yourself lucky I don't exclude you from school straight away, young lady. Don't dig your grave.'

I have a sudden vision of myself in the middle of a cemetery at midnight heaving spade after spade of soil up, bones and skulls everywhere, with Auntie Astonished standing over me. It's pouring with rain and Auntie Astonished is saying, 'Dig, liar! Dig!'

'Until you write the letter, you will stay in Isolation. If you haven't written it by the end of today, your parents will be informed and you will be back in Isolation tomorrow.'

'But why should I write an apology for something...'

'Stop,' the Head snaps. 'This is how this ends, Adele. The letter. Write it. Now get to Isolation and write. I will phone through to tell them to expect you and provide you with pen and paper.'

Isolation is a boring room with books, a rattling radiator and one window. There's some Year 7 kid who smells of wee in one corner, but nobody else except the Teaching Assistant. I take a desk by the window. I can't believe Mikaela has done the dirty on me like this.

I watch the playground through the window. People point at me and hold their hands up to their mouths, whispering. I realise I am The Racist. My mind starts spinning. The way the playground works, by the end of the day the whispers will be saying I called Mikaela every racist name under the sun. From most popular girl in the class, I'll be the one nobody picks to do anything with. Mikaela will be loving it.

The tears start. I turn away from the girl who smells of wee. I don't want her to see I'm upset. I won't give in though. They can keep me in Isolation for the rest of the year before I write the letter.

Time drags.

The Teaching Assistant comes over just before lunch and asks if I need some help or a dictionary or maybe I would like some tips on how to phrase some words of regret. I slump onto the desk with my eyes closed. He gets the message and goes away.

I count the flower pattern on the wallpaper and the number of floor tiles in the room.

If Mikaela wanted to hurt me, she's doing a good job.

Lunchtime is hardest. A dinner lady brings dinner to me. She smiles at me so nicely.

In the afternoon, a Year 11 joins us in Isolation. She's got a bandaged arm. She leans on the wall and pulls down the bandage. There are fresh cuts all along her arm. She smiles at them, then pulls the bandage up again. It's the "in" thing to cut yourself in Year 11. I imagine lifting a knife at lunchtime while in Isolation, then doing a small cut. Watching the blood bead. Maybe leaning against the wall with the goth girl as I do it. I show her. She then shows me her own forearm, criss-crossed with longer, deeper cuts, smiles loftily and moves away from me. I shrug the thought off. I don't fancy cutting myself.

Twice Mrs Duras comes in to check whether I've written anything. Twice she goes away disappointed.

I look at the paper. I pick up the pen. The Teaching Assistant's shoulders twitch.

I write the date. Then "Dear Mikaela".

I can't bring myself to write any more. I won't write something that's not true.

Time passes slowly. A Teaching Assistant strolls over, glances, and then strolls back to his desk again.

I remember when I was eight, bouncing on a trampoline at a friend's birthday party. We all sat down afterwards in one big row and plaited one another's hair. Mum and Dad were sitting around a patio table chatting. The sun was streaming through tall, wavy trees. After, there were pillow fights, torches, karaoke and prawn cocktail crisps. I want to be that girl again.

I stare at the page. "Dear Mikaela". I've added doodles of tall, wavy trees under that.

The Teaching Assistant picks the paper up at the end of the day and tut-tuts.

At home time, they make me wait till the playground has cleared. I leave school blinking back tears.

I write a text to Mikaela: *u stpd btch y u doin this 2 me.* But I click Delete instead of Send. I'm not allowed to have any contact with her. I get home and there is an answering machine message. It's from the Head. She's "seriously concerned by a racial incident involving your daughter" and asks that someone phone her back ASAP. I delete it.

Mum's in bed, sleeping. She looks OK.

I phone Marcus. He picks up on the sixth ring. I can tell from his tone that he doesn't really want to listen to me. It's all 'um' and 'yeh' and 'you do whatever you think is right.' Maybe it's a bad line and he's not hearing me well, but more likely he's in the middle of his homework and he can't be bothered with my problems. I end the call thinking maybe even he doubts me because when I said to him, 'I never said "black bitch", I said "sad bitch"' he hesitated before saying, 'of course'. Why did he hesitate?

Tuesday morning arrives and I force myself to get ready for school. Dad drives me. Another eight hours of Isolation. To think Dad's paying for me to sit in an empty room staring at walls, listening to silence, sniffing wee. Or maybe he isn't. He had that strange conversation about school fees at the match, I remember. I thought Dad was loaded. What's going on there? I look across and almost ask him, but Dad's still thunder-faced. His hands are clenching

126

the steering wheel. Water eases down my cheek from my eyes. I don't bother wiping it away.

'Serves you right for being such a stupid girl,' Dad says.

Dad thinks I'm crying about the shoplifting. He never has a clue what I'm upset about. At least that hasn't changed. I stop crying.

We're at a traffic light.

'You'll get over it, Adele,' Dad says. And I realise he's crying a little bit too.

My phone buzzes. Mikaela's sent me a text. I don't open it.

Dad drops me a street away from school so he doesn't get stuck in traffic and I walk the last hundred metres. When I get there, Mikaela is at the gates, waiting. She's with her mum, who starts waving. I walk up to them, scared. Mikaela's mum's got this intense look on her face. Mikaela's studying her shoes.

'Hello, Mrs Robinson,' I say cautiously.

'Good morning, Adele,' she says. 'Looking forward to school?'

I shrug. She obviously doesn't know I'm in Isolation all day.

There's a pause. I'm about to start walking again when Mikaela's mum nudges Mikaela. 'Mikaela, do you have something to say?'

It's an order, not a question, from her mum.

'Sorry,' says Mikaela.

'Say it louder,' her mum demands.

'I'm sorry, Adele.'

'Why? Look her in the eye and say why.'

Mikaela drags her eyes up to look at me. 'I should never of let them accuse you of being a racist. I knew you didn't say those words. I was just upset and I wanted to hurt you.'

'That's better,' her mum tells her. 'It's unforgiveable, Mikaela. We black people fought for so long against racism. We went to jail, even died for that cause. How dare you use racism as a weapon, just because you were upset. Doing something like that damages not just Adele, it damages the entire cause, black people everywhere. Understand?'

I almost say, yes, but it's Mikaela who says yes. She's crying.

'It's OK,' I say, mainly to Mikaela. 'We all do things when we're angry.'

'It's no excuse,' Mrs Robinson says. 'It's not acceptable. Hand her the note, Mikaela.'

Mikaela rummages in her bag.

As Mikaela looks for it, Mrs Robinson says, 'I heard the Head was asking you to write a note of apology. We have no secrets, me and Mikaela. She told me. A note of apology has been written. But by the correct person. Mikaela?'

Mikaela hands me a piece of paper. It has her handwriting on it.

'Will you accept this apology, Adele?'

I nod. Mikaela is bawling. I stroke her arm. 'Don't cry, Mikay,' I say. 'It's OK.'

Mrs Robinson herself sniffles. 'You girls... Now one last thing, Adele.'

'Yes, Mrs Robinson?'

'Mikaela tells me everything, you follow?'

I nod.

'And I know you were caught shoplifting. And that you had invited Mikaela along that day.'

It's my turn to look at my shoes.

'There are some rumours that Mikaela was involved. I've listened to her and I have taken the advice of a criminal lawyer. She may have been with you during your ...' Mrs Robinson searches for the right word. 'Activities,' she finally decides upon. 'But as far as the evidence shows, she never took anything outside of the store and she had no knowledge that such a thing was going to be attempted. That is a fair conclusion from the evidence available. It would absolutely ruin her prospects if anything to the contrary were to gain ground and I will not allow it. Did you see her steal anything, Adele?'

'No,' I say.

'Are you certain she was aware of what you were planning to do?'

'No,' I say. I am certain, but it's also clear that Mrs Robinson wants me to say no.

'Thank you, Adele.' Then, 'This new Head had better watch out making wild accusations. I don't know where she got the notion from. Mikaela and I have an appointment with her this morning. You may be called in. I will expect you to say the same thing you have just told me.'

I nod. 'Of course.'

'Apologise once more to Adele, Mikaela.'

'Sorry,' Mikaela mumbles.

I am counting the number of ants retrieving bread crumbs from Floor Tile Twenty Seven in Isolation when the Teaching Assistant tells me the Head wants to see me in her office. I can't help a slow smile as I walk along the corridor.

The green light is already on. I knock, open Auntie Astonished's door and go in. Mikaela and her mum are sitting there already. Auntie Astonished has the same stuff on her desk as last time. The atmosphere is different though.

'Take a seat, Adele,' the Head simpers.

I sit. The Head looks likes she's been beaten up badly by Mrs Robinson, who, even though she's sitting down, looks like a boxer on her toes, ready to lay into anyone who steps out of line.

'I have just received this note from Mikaela,' the Head says, through gritted teeth.

I look dutifully curious.

'And it exonerates you completely, Adele, of the racist remark Mikaela had previously accused you of.'

'She didn't accuse her,' Mikaela's mum intervenes, 'She simply did not correct what others said.'

'Be that as it may,' the Head says, irritated. 'Of course, you two girls could have concocted this note to get Adele out of trouble.'

Mikaela's mum is about to say something but the Head presses on quickly:

'However, the school has a thorough process when we investigate these things. I have received written statements from the children who witnessed the incident and, although there are some contradictions, those statements suggest that the word used was "sad" and not "black". Is that right, Adele?'

I nod. Finally the truth is out.

'In that case, Adele has been wronged,' the Head says, 'not least by myself, and I ... I apologise to you, Adele.'

I enjoy watching the Head squirm. She wrings her hands. '...And I will ensure that your class and the whole school know that the allegation was simply not true.'

'Thank you,' I say.

After a few more lemon-sucking statements from the Head, including that I no longer have to be in Isolation, I am dismissed.

At lunchtime, Mikaela comes running up to me in the playground. She says the Head apologised to her and her mum for thinking she went shoplifting.

I feel guilty that I snitched on her to the Head, but since Mikaela doesn't know I snitched, and she got away with it, it doesn't count, I decide. Me and Mikaela sit together in the dining room. People point and whisper. Me and Mikaela tell anyone who asks it was all a mistake, and we're best friends again.

On Wednesday morning the Form Teacher tells the whole class I said 'silly sad bitch' and not 'silly black bitch'. Everyone then has to join hands and listen to a Martin Luther King speech. Someone objects they are not allowed to listen to religious speeches but the Form Teacher says it's not religious, it's spiritual and there's a difference. So the whole class joins hands and listens to Martin Luther King's 'I Have A Dream'. It's OK, though it's a bit long. We end with a compulsory group hug. The school day ends with PE and the team sheet for Saturday's semi-final with St Cuthbert's. At last, there's some good news. Both my name and Mikaela's are up there at the top of the sheet.

CHAPTER 16

FIVE SECONDS, WITH TONGUES

It's Saturday morning and Dad is driving me to St Cuthbert's, a Catholic school in the city centre. It's his birthday. His presents were cufflinks (MTB), bow tie (me) and two tickets to a rock concert to see Mum's favourite band (Mum). He's humming along to the radio.

'Dad, I love it when you're happy.'

'So do I. I'm sorry I've been a bit grumpy. Work's been tough.'

The air con is on max. At first I think that's why Dad's grimacing, but then I notice it's the jaw-lock grimace he does when he's about to say something difficult. I wait.

'I've checked and the school can't expel you for the shoplifting. Under their own rules, they can only judge you on how you behave at school.'

'Thanks, Dad,' I reply. It's a weird thing for Dad to say and I'm impressed that he actually cares about me enough to hunt down the school rules and find all that out. People are confusing. You want to hate them and then they say or do something that makes it impossible.

We leave the car in a multi-storey car park, walk across

a square and arrive at the St Cuthbert gatehouse. A security guard lets us through. It's a seriously religious school. The front gardens have a statue of the Virgin Mary and there's a huge wooden cross hung above the school building entrance. A nun in a grey uniform crosses the garden and shepherds us through the school building to the field at the rear where the changing rooms are. At any moment I expect to come across a host of levitating nuns. Dad is amazed the school owns a football pitch in the city centre and says the land value must be through the roof. He spots Mrs Robinson at the pitch edge and, with a little kiss, shoos me to go and get changed.

Everyone in our dressing room is quiet because the home team are reciting the Lord's Prayer next door. It's weird. Nobody wants to interrupt. Even Miss Fridge, who is a devout atheist, gazes quietly at the ceiling fan.

Finally, we trot out. I study the touchline. Faye White isn't there. Miss Fridge said they don't always send the same scout and we should all play like there is an England scout out there somewhere.

The match starts. Maybe the nuns got rugby and football mixed up. St Cuthbert's come flying at us with arms, legs and knees. I get hauled down twice as I race for the ball. Mikaela gets pushed over. The referee blows twenty times in the first five minutes. I look over at Dad. He's standing with Mrs Robinson, gobsmacked. He does the sign of a cross at me from the touchline. Sometimes my dad's funny. Just sometimes. Finally the referee calls the coach nun over. The two of them huddle for a minute, then the coach nun calls her team to her.

The match restarts and this time they don't foul us. Mikaela floats a beautiful ball high up. I bounce it off my shin and wallop it into the net. 1–0. We get our second goal from a corner kick that Mikaela takes. It bends all the way into the net without anyone touching it. Our third is a crazy own goal when their defenders pass the ball back too quickly for their goalkeeper. I look over at Dad. He's laughing, so is Mikaela's mum who is steadying Dad's shoulders because he's laughing so much. The two of them stagger away from the touchline, laughing together.

Mikaela runs to the side of the pitch near me. I ask her what's up. She says she needs a tampon. The referee runs over and Miss Fridge explains Mikaela's problem. I expect to see Mikaela's mum in the huddle but she's nowhere on the touchline, neither is Dad. The ref nods to Miss Fridge and lets Mikaela chase over to the changing room with her bag.

I drop back into midfield, taking Mikaela's place there for a while. St Cuthbert's start to fancy their chances. Against ten, they are almost good, in a kick-and-rush kind of way. We're clinging on, throwing ourselves at the ball to stop them getting a shooting opportunity.

Finally, Mikaela's back. She flings her bag down at the touchline and comes running onto the pitch. Something's wrong. She slams in a high tackle, upending a St Cuthbert's midfielder. The referee waves a yellow card at her. Miss Fridge shouts, 'Mikaela! Mikaela!' but Mikaela's doesn't hear her. I go over to her. Her eyes are full of hate and she pushes me away. She charges into a tackle again and wins the ball. Instead of passing it to me she belts it high into the sky. I look over at Miss Fridge. She's on the touchline, livid. My dad's there as well, standing with Mrs Robinson. It's weird neither of them are saying anything to Mikaela. Mikaela elbows me in the ribs as she runs past me.

'Hey!'

She ignores me. The ball is at her feet. She's looking over at the touchline. Suddenly she smacks the ball low and hard, straight at my dad. It hits his goolies and he crumples up in agony. I tear over to her.

'What was that?' I shout at her.

'Bring it!' she dares me.

Fine. I grab her. She's got a knee in my ribs and I've sunk my nails into her neck. Then my dad and Mrs Robinson are pulling us apart. I'm panting. The ref waves two red cards. Mikaela's still wind-milling her arms and lashing at my dad with her feet. Miss Fridge wrenches her off the field by the waist. I realise then that Miss Fridge is not fat, she's all muscle – she flips Mikaela so easily. Miss Fridge frogmarches us to the changing rooms. She's ranting and raving as she hauls us away, but I'm not listening, I'm wondering what came over Mikaela and whether we're going to lose the match now. It's the semi-final. I wanted a medal. And what if the England scout was there?

In the changing rooms, Miss Fridge sits us down. She takes a deep breath then says she has to get back to the match, and don't we dare fight again, because she will personally kill us if we do.

Mikaela's lost her rage. She sits on the bench looking sad and floppy.

'Well?' I ask her, when her breathing steadies.

She does her cow eyes look at me.

'What is it?'

'Those wet punches, Adele. You're getting soft,' she says, sniffling.

'Well, your headlocks aren't what they used to be, Mikay.'

She flicks away tears.

'Tell me,' I say softly.

We're sat on the same bench. The showers are hissing even though there's no-one in them.

Mikaela takes a deep breath then it all comes out in a big gush: 'I went to put in my tampon and while I was here, my phone rang, it was my auntie and she wants to talk to my mum, she says it's urgent and I need to hand my phone to her right now, she's not picking up her own, so I go to find my mum only she's meant to be on the touchline and she's not. That's when I caught them behind a tree. Kissing.'

She looks over at me like that's the end of the world. 'Who?' I ask.

She stares at me hard.

I shrug. 'They've kissed before. In the car park at Parents Evening, remember?'

Mikaela shakes her head. 'Not like this. I filmed it.'

She takes out her phone and strokes up a video. I lean in with Mikaela. There's lots of blur, then two heads. Mikaela's mum's shoes. The camera jumps up. They're in a kiss, definitely a kiss. And it's at least five seconds. With tongues. Dad has his hands cupping Mrs Robinson's face and she's on tiptoes, face turned up, sucking his face off. They break apart suddenly and the video goes blurred. You just hear one word, 'Mikaela!' shouted by her mum. Then the video freezes.

136

'See?' says Mikaela.

It's my dad alright. Unless someone coshed him on the head, stole his clothes and copied his hair cut.

'Did you know?'

I'm too stunned to speak.

'You didn't.'

'Mikaela I'm so sorry,' I say. My mind is all over the place. I remember now my dad pulling us apart. Yet he wasn't going nuts at Mikaela for firing the ball at him. And Mrs Robinson never said anything either. Maybe they were too ashamed after Mikaela had caught them at it.

Mikaela's playing the video on loop, as if by watching it she can somehow change what happens. She turns to me, eyes all watery and blurts, 'I mean, your frigging dad, Adele!'

Then she throws her boots down in the changing room. They skid to a wall.

I don't know what to do, or say. I can tell, with the mood she's in, Mikaela's going to fight me again if she can, so I get up and leave. I don't even turn to say goodbye.

Dad's outside the changing room.

'Adele?' he says, 'What was that all about?'

'Don't bother, Dad,' I tell him, brushing past. I can see Mikaela's mum, lurking by a floppy tree. *Funny, she's not rushing to see Mikaela*, I think.

'What about my birthday?' he calls, running up beside me – making a joke of it.

I stop. 'Dad, leave me alone.'

He's more serious now. 'Was it what Mikaela saw? It's not what you think. You're jumping to conclusions.'

I don't want to talk to him right now. I start running. Nobody can keep up with me when I run.

He gives up. 'Suit yourself,' he calls out to my back.

When I reach the checkpoint, I glance back. My dad's huddled up with Mikaela's mum by the floppy tree. They're leaning into each other.

I walk across town to the bus stop. On the way, I get asked a million things by chuggers – to go for a pizza, to sign up for a charity, to buy tickets for clubbing and to donate to orphans of Afghanistan. I brush my way past all of them.

On the bus I think about the kiss. Was it really that bad? It is Dad's birthday. Maybe it was a birthday kiss. Or a bit of fooling around. The two of them don't add up. Dad is an out and out racist when he's tired or drunk. My dad doesn't make sense. People don't make sense. The human species doesn't make sense. I bring up Facebook and find out we won the match 3–2.

Mikaela has PM'd me:

Ms Fridge sez we bannd from Englnd trials. Hv a nice day.

So an England scout was there.

I get home, dump my boots in my boots bucket and check on Mum. She's not in. Neither is my brother. Or Dad. I tidy the kitchen then go back upstairs, slam my door, flop on my bed and beat the mattress with my fists.

When I'm finished with that, I look around. Everything in my room looks sad. The chairs, the mirror, the trophy cabinet, the curtains, the boots bucket, the keyboard and the toy zebra I've had since I was eight. Even my boots, soaking in their bucket. What use are they now? It was my boots that brought Dad to the games. My boots were how he met Mikaela's mum. My boots have ruined everything. I can never like football the same way again ever, I decide. Everything's spoiled. Everything's ruined.

I go downstairs and make toast. Dad comes in. He stands in the kitchen doorway, wordless.

'Why, Dad?' I ask him.

He shuffles his feet. 'You're reading too much into it. It's my birthday, it was a kiss.' He says it like someone stuck a stamp on an envelope for him.

'No, Dad. It was on the lips and with tongues. For ages. Mikaela filmed it. Don't you like Mum anymore?'

He runs his hands through his hair. 'You're reading too much into it, kid,' he says again. He's treating it like it's all a joke. He gets out the orange juice carton from the fridge.

'Are you a cheating bastard like Miss Richards says all men are?' I say.

'Get real, Adele,' he says, still calm. He nudges a kitchen chair out with his thigh, sinks into it and glugs on the orange juice for a few seconds. Then he looks at me. I look back, waiting.

'OK, I kissed her. She gave me a big "happy birthday" kiss. So what? I'm Italian. I'm hot-blooded. I need love. And I don't mean the physical stuff that men and women do.'

'Sex?' I ask. Dad's never been comfortable saying the word in front of me.

'Yes. I'm not talking about sex. I need someone to say "Vincent, I enjoy having a conversation with you, I enjoy your company, I believe in your dreams." You understand,

Zowie?'

'You just called me Zowie.'

'Did I?' Dad sighs.

'Maybe you need to be having this conversation with Mum?'

Suddenly Dad looks ancient. He rubs his rubbery forehead. 'Listen, there was nothing going on. We are a family, Adele. OK, we're not a "sit around a picnic in a field holding hands" kind of family, but we are a family and I wouldn't risk that. I love you all. You, your mum, Anthony. I'd never want to leave you, you mean everything to me. I wouldn't risk that for a quick roll in the hay with Lydia. Or anybody else.'

'If you're leaving, I'm staying here with Mum.'

'I'm not leaving. Where did you get that from?'

Dad drinks off all the OJ and tosses the carton at the bin, basketball style. It misses. 'I just would like, sometimes, to feel like I'm not just some giant cash machine on legs. I'd like someone to understand *my* problems, occasionally.'

'I'm not meant to understand your problems, Dad. You're my dad, you're supposed to understand *my* problems.'

'I'm trying, Adele. You don't know how hard I've been trying. I mean...'

'Tell me then.'

'I can't.'

'Why? Because I'm too young? Because I'm a girl? Why?'

'It's not any of that, it's... Not everything can be solved by being talked about.'

'But I want to know, Dad. I mean, do you even love me?'

'Don't be stupid. Of course I do. Why do you say that?'

140

'You don't show any interest in me.'

I can't believe I'm having this heart to heart with Dad.

'I'm moving heaven and earth for you, Adele, you just don't see it.'

'You drive me to school, Dad. Big deal.'

'Yes, I drive you to school. And I've been going to your matches.'

'I'm not the reason you're there.'

'How can you say that? And you don't know the arses I've licked trying to get you a sponsorship deal.'

Dad goes to ask a question, then stops.

'What?' I ask him.

'This kiss. Have you told your mum?'

I shake my head.

'Good.'

'What kiss?' MTB has arrived. He must have sneaked in. He throws his sports bag down on the kitchen floor in a huge wave of boy energy.

'Tony,' says Dad, hauling himself up and moving MTB's bag out of the middle of the kitchen floor. 'Tony, Tony, Tony, just leave it, yeah? Just leave it. Adele, come here.'

I go over to Dad.

He takes me in his arms and squeezes me. Tightly, like he's never squeezed me before, then kisses me on the top of my head.

'Tony, here.'

MTB looks across at me as Dad kisses my brother's forehead while hugging us both. MTB's eyes are saying, *what's going on here?*

'Happy birthday, Dad,' MTB says. 'I love you too.'

'Yeh, happy birthday,' I say. 'I love you no matter what.'

'Love you both,' he says. 'Now I've got to make some phone calls.'

Dad leaves the kitchen.

As soon as he's gone, MTB laughs. 'A kiss? You mean he doesn't know about you and Marcus? And he thinks Mum doesn't know? He's so out of touch, isn't he? He should be checking you two are using condoms.'

I throw the empty orange juice carton at MTB and run upstairs to my room.

My phone goes off. It's Mikaela. I take a deep breath then answer.

'My dad says it was just a kiss,' I tell her, before she says anything.

'They probably talked about it and that's what they've decided to say to us. I know your dad's aftershave, Adele, and I've smelt it on Mum before.'

'Just because your mum smells of Armani doesn't mean it's my dad.'

There's silence on the other end of the phone.

'I mean, is she getting any from your dad? I've heard that if they don't get it from their partner they go elsewhere.'

'Who is "they" and what is "it"?'

'You know.'

'...I can't believe you, Adele!'

'I didn't mean it like that. Mikaela. Wait! Mikaela! It came out wrong.'

More silence.

'You're like a sister to me, Mikay. I don't want to lose you as a friend. Mikaela?'

142

Finally she speaks. Her voice is ice. 'This situation is very fucked up, Adele. Just try and keep your dad away from my mum, OK? My dad has just moved back in and I want it to stay that way.'

I go to speak but she ends the call.

I don't know what to do. I'm losing my best friend ever and I can't do anything about it. And what's this about her dad moving back in? Does that mean her mum and my dad are, like Dad says, just friends? Nothing makes sense. I've managed to pummel a great big dish into the middle of the mattress when my phone bleeps. This time it's Marcus.

Wot u doin

Nuffin much

Why dnt u call rnd mine

If u ask nicely

Pls

Maybe. wait & c

CHAPTER 17

TATTOO YOU

I phone a taxi and ask the driver to get me to Marcus's as fast as he can. I'm about to tap on his front door when his mum bursts out with Leah in her arms and two bulging bags in her hands. Leah's wailing. She sees me, stops wailing long enough to break out a big smile, then goes back to wailing.

'Hi love, just grab that other bag for me will you?' Marcus's mum, says, 'the one in the hallway. My box of tricks.'

I pick the bag up and follow her to her car.

'Hold her a moment,' she says. She pours a wailing Leah into my arms then goes to open the driveway gates. Leah grabs hold of my thumb and pushes it into her mouth. For about two seconds she's quiet as she sucks desperately. Then she starts wailing again.

'If she has any more she'll throw up,' Marcus's mum says, peeling Leah off me. She straps Leah into the car seat then puts the car in gear.

I wave them both off. The front door is open. I go in.

Marcus comes galloping down the stairs. He's wearing about half a bottle of after-shave.

'Your mum let me in,' I explain.

'She's off to Magic Circle,' Marcus says, shaking his head. He nods for me to follow him inside.

From the living room I can see his dad in the back garden hanging out washing. I sit on the sofa. The clock says ten past one.

'Don't get comfortable, Dad wants me outside,' Marcus says. 'He's got a guy coming round showing him how to set up an Ebay shop.' He shouts this last bit from the kitchen where I can hear him opening the fridge door.

'What's he gonna sell?' I call out.

There's no answer. It doesn't surprise me. Marcus's ears aren't good and he won't have heard me.

He comes back in. 'What was that?'

'What's your dad gonna sell on Ebay?'

'Stuff,' Marcus shrugs. He grabs his jacket from the coat hooks under the stairs. 'Right, we're off.' He pats his pockets. 'One sec.'

He spins out into the back garden. He comes back two minutes later with a twenty pound note in his hand and a grin on his face. 'Now we're rolling!'

We wander through Marcus's neighbourhood. He has a ball at his feet. I'm calming down from the fight with Mikaela and being kicked off the England team and Dad and his stupid kiss with Mrs Robinson. Marcus does the flip-flap then the step-over. Some kids gather to watch. He's such a show-off. He kicks the ball over to me. I do a few moves, nowhere near as smart as his. People gasp, mainly because I'm a girl. I whack the ball back to Marcus. He peels off some headers then drops the ball into his arms. 'Show's over!' he says to the local urchins. They slope off.

We walk on, Marcus juggling the ball low. For a moment I want him to stop juggling and hold my hand, but then I don't care. I think about how life is and I decide I don't care about not being on the England team. Why should I, when no-one else cares? Mrs Richards is right. It would only matter if I was a boy. Nobody really cares about girl's football, nobody comes knocking on your door trying to sign you up for Manchester United or anything. Compare that with boys. Boys are instant heroes the moment they can do a few tricks. I tell this to Marcus. Then I tell him about the fight with Mikaela and how we've been banned from the England trials.

He finally stops juggling. 'What were you fighting about?'

'She thinks my dad's having an affair with her mum. She saw them kissing.'

'A kiss is not an affair.'

'A five second kiss, with tongues?'

Marcus shrugs. 'When my dad was a club singer women used to come up to him and snog his face off every night. Mum didn't bat an eyelid. It was just part of the job. Show business.'

'My dad's a banker, not a singer.'

'Yeh,' he agrees. 'True.' He thinks a bit. 'A five second kiss?'

I nod.

'But no ... roving hands?'

I shake my head.

'That's more than a kiss. And yet...'

My phone rings. I shush Marcus.

It's MC. I mouth 'MC Banshee' to Marcus. He frowns.
MC's buzzing.

'I'm with Cakes. You coming lifting? It's a hot day for it.
A rob for one is a rob for all!'

Marcus is shaking his head.

'I can't go. I'm with someone.'

'You don't want to get on the wrong side of me, Adele.
You've got a pretty nose, it won't look good squashed into
your face.'

'Sorry.'

'You're chicken aren't you? Just 'cos you got caught.'

'I'll ring you back.' I end the call.

Marcus is right in my face. 'Don't even think about it,'
he says.

I break free of him. 'What *are* we going to do then?' I
ask. 'I'm bored. And wet.'

There's been a sudden gale. It's blown off now but it's left
us soaked. We're in a corner shop doorway.

'Not thieving,' Marcus says. 'I'll think of something.'

He takes us to a high street. It's a sound mashup of car
horns, road drills, Bangla CD's blasting out of shopfronts,
and 'Buy your phonecards' shouts from the phonecard stall
guys. We pass restaurants and take-aways and stop outside
a furniture store that's selling gold-sprayed bed frames.
Marcus points to a sign hanging above the shop. *Tattoo You*
it says, with an arrow pointing upwards. I look at him.

'Nooooo!'

'Let's do it!'

He grabs my hand and we race up a creaky staircase.
It's lined with print-outs of tattoo designs. Swords. Snakes.

Dragons. Devils. Microphones. Eyes. Eagles. Virgin Marys. Naked Ladies. Butterflies. Hearts. Lions. Anchors. Everything leaps out at once. Marcus pulls me up the last flight of stairs.

The studio doorway is framed by two silver skulls and a Jolly Roger flag. There's a plastic bead curtain and behind that a waiting room the size of a telephone box. We squeeze in and this triggers a bell. We wait. We're so close Marcus is giggling because our bellies are rubbing together. Someone draws a bolt back and the upper part of a door in the wall facing us opens. A woman with straggly black hair and breasts laced into a sleeveless black dress that shows off weird pattern tattoos on her shoulders appears from behind this half-door. She looks us up and down, then says, 'Piss off!'

'We've got money,' pleads Marcus. He flashes his twenty pound note.

'Underage,' she says, 'not worth my licence. Go on, do one.'

'We'll pay double,' I say. Marcus nudges me. I nudge him back. He forgets I've got money too.

'And don't come back, Romeo and frogging Juliet, or my foot's gonna tattoo your arses.'

We are so close to the tattoo lady that we smell each word she says. 'Arses' smelt of hard-boiled eggs. Marcus brushes aside the bead curtain. 'Come on,' he says, 'fuck her.'

'Yeh, fuck you!' I tell Miss Tattoo as I step out with him. She looks at me like, *is that all you've got?* And gives us both the middle finger, slowly.

148

We tumble down the stairs in a fit of giggles.

The gale has stopped and the sun's blazing. I spot a big plastic sheet across the road, sheltering a shop's fruits and vegetables. It's bulging with rain water. I dart across the road. Marcus dashes after me. Before he can stop me I've found a pole and whacked the plastic. A ton of water shoots down off the plastic, drenching me, Marcus and three gasping shoppers.

'Run!' Marcus shouts.

We run like the wind.

We make it to a patch of grass at the end of the parade of shops and sit on a bench there.

'What are you like?' says Marcus. 'You just do things.'

'Fun though, no?'

'Whatever.'

Marcus has taken his hearing aids out and is wiping them. He pops them back in then gets up and starts juggling his ball.

'Do you sleep with it?' I ask him.

He doesn't answer but a grin sneaks out of one side of his mouth.

'Admit it, Marky, you sleep with your football!'

'Shh,' he says, 'I'm trying to land this.'

'Boring!'

He's doing a spin round and trap. As usual when he starts with his tricks, a crowd builds up. I wait till he kicks the ball really high, then spring up and grab it.

'What do you do that for?' he says, trying to wrestle the ball from me.

I hang on to it and he smothers me in his arms, which is

kind of nice. 'Come on, let's go,' I say, almost licking his ear. He pulls away me. I bounce the ball back to him.

Where did the time go? It's nearly eight o'clock and we're both hungry. We've ended up back at Marcus's. His dad's out at a recording studio. His mum's in the kitchen. Baby Leah is sleeping in her buggy and his mum says not to get her out of it because that will wake her. Marcus is in the back alley practicing half volleys. It's weird sitting in someone else's house, in a room alone. The TV is blaring out a game show. The house phone rings and I wonder whether I should pick it up. Just as I get up, it stops ringing. There's photos all along the mantelpiece, mainly of Marcus when he was younger, some of Leah. There is one that I guess is his mum and dad billions of years ago. They're arm in arm, leaning against a car. She's got flares and a tie dye top, he's got a big Afro, a tight T shirt and muscles. There's a small photo of an old man looking regal in a gold frame in the middle of the mantelpiece. The face is more like Marcus than his dad. I pick it up. People say sometimes genes skip a generation. And sometimes they don't. I think, *what if I become my dad, with his temper? Or my mum, all druggy and dreamy?* Both thoughts scare me.

'That's his granddad,' Marcus's mum says, bursting in, her arms full of laundry.

Her voice makes Leah stir. Marcus's mum freezes and puts a finger to her lips. Leah's little hands are up and jerking. Gradually they relax and drop to her legs again. Her mum takes a step. The floor creaks. Leah opens one groggy eye. The one eye looks up at her mum who stays as still as a statue. The eye looks around the room. Will she go

150

back to sleep? We're both holding our breath. Leah's one eye fixes on me. A second eye joins the first. Both eyes stare at me as only babies' eyes can, intently and completely blank, like maybe she's dreaming with her eyes open. I count four seconds, not breathing. Then the sound wave hits.

'Waaahhhh!' goes Leah.

'That's all I need!' her mum says, dumping the laundry on the sofa. She unstraps Leah, gives her a big blubbery kiss, changes her nappy, tickles her tum, feeds her with a bottle, and then pours her into my arms. She's lovely and warm and smells of soap and talc.

'Have you burped a baby before?' her mum asks.

'What's that?'

She shows me. Soon I'm doing little circular motions on Leah's back. Leah gurgles.

'That's a burp,' her mum says. 'Keep that going while I put this laundry away. I won't be two ticks.'

Half an hour later, I'm still holding Leah. She's bouncing up and down in my arms. Marcus barges back in via the kitchen. He's all muddy and he's chuffed with himself.

'You should of seen me land the volleys. Boom boom boom! Dead centre every time!'

'I wish I had a baby sister. Leah's so cute,' I say, as Leah starts kicking, then wriggles across into her brother's arms. He takes her up.

'Try changing her nappy,' he says, sniffing her. His mum plucks Leah off him.

'Can I stay tonight?' I ask.

Marcus's mum turns and looks at me squint-eyed.

I can't believe what I've just said either.

151

Marcus wriggles in his shoes.

'I could sleep in Leah's room!' I add quickly.

'Marcus, did you put her up to this?' his mum quizzes.

'No! Why does everything have to be me!' Marcus protests.

His mum looks at me kindly. 'I'm not being funny, love, but, why would you want to stay here? Your house is a lot less cramped.'

'Here's warmer,' I say. 'And I could help out with Leah.'

'Adele, is there anything wrong at home?'

I shrug. 'Mum and Dad aren't getting on that well so...'

'Her dad's having an affair!' Marcus blurts out.

I elbow him.

'What was that for?'

'Oh jeez, you kids,' mutters Mrs Adenuga, then, 'Adele, get your mum on the phone for me.'

I dial my mum. After five failed attempts, I text her:

pik up the fone u dozy cow its me

When I next ring, she answers.

'Don't be calling me a dozy cow, I'm your mother and you have no idea of the things I do...'

I let Mum blab on till she has to come up for air.

'Mum, can I stay at Marcus's?'

That sets her off on another six hour speech:

'I don't even allow your brother to... You could be out all night for all I know, and even if you weren't, I mean, hello, you're only fourteen. You're too young. I hardly know the boy. He could be an escaped murderer. You could get

152

pregnant. You don't have a toothbrush ... I suppose it's better you're out of the way.'

'What do you mean "out of the way"?' I ask.

'Nothing ... I don't feel comfortable about this, Adele.'

'So that's a "yes" then, Mum?'

'Pass me the phone, Adele,' says Marcus's mum.

I hand her the phone. Mrs Adenuga talks with her. I get her side of the conversation:

'No, me neither... About 6 months ... yes, they're just kids ... Mm. They do get on well together ... He has his moments but he's no angel either ... Exactly, in my days ... It's ... Marcus? Of course ... I'll make sure ... If he tries, I'll chop it off myself ... Not so much spare, it's the baby's room ... Very well actually, you'd be surprised, it's actually sweet to see ... Maybe she hides it ... Yes ... I know, I know ... No ... Don't you worry, there'll be no sneaking around, I'll put tacks in the hallway! Any concerns you just ring me any time. Let me give you our house number.'

I can tell things are running our way. I look over to Marcus. His dimple grin is on full. I show him my crossed fingers.

His mum hands me back the phone. 'Your mum wants to speak to you.'

Mum's got her posh voice on, like she thinks maybe my phone's on speaker.

'We need words when you get back tomorrow,' she says.

'Thanks, Mum, I love you.'

'I love you too, Adele. And I'm really, really sorry about what I said when you broke the window.'

I say nothing. I don't want to go into it.

'... But we still need words, Adele.'

'Will you cook lasagne tomorrow?'

'Behave yourself and don't show me up. We brought you up right, don't embarrass us.'

Marcus's mum is leaning in trying to overhear, but politely, like I'm not supposed to notice. 'That's really nice, Mum, use lots of tomatoes.'

'Are you listening?'

'I'm just polishing my halo.'

'What?'

'Jeez, Mum. I'll behave, OK? Love you. Bye.' I press End Call.

Marcus's mum looks at me, dead serious. 'You'll be in Leah's room, you understand?'

I nod.

'No sneaking round in the middle of the night, either of you. Marcus?'

'Right,' Marcus scowls.

'Right,' I nod. 'Does he need feeding in the middle of the night?'

'Him? Not usually,' Marcus's mum snorts.

I go red. 'I meant she. Leah.'

She shakes her head. 'But she does wake up sometimes. Just ignore her and she'll go back to sleep. Whatever you do don't take her out of the cot, because then you'll never get her back in. I'll go and sort out the spare bed.'

'Do you need any help?' I ask.

'No, you chill down here, sweetheart, I'll take care of it.'

She goes upstairs. Marcus looks at me, then quickly away, then at me again.

154

'This is weird,' he says.

'Good weird?'

'Yeh.' He's amused and embarrassed and excited all at once. So am I.

'Erm, I'll go and get you some pyjamas,' he says.

He goes off. Two minutes later, he's down with stuff in his arms that he pushes into mine.

I take a look. It's a monkey print onesie. I bite my lip trying not to laugh. I'm imagining him in them.

'What?' he says.

'No, they're ... cute,' I say.

His mum bustles in. 'They're his favourite ones. He must really like you,' his mum says, smirking.

'Shut up, Mum,' Marcus says.

'They look really warm,' I say, 'You're definitely my go-to guy for PJs.' I kiss him lightly on the cheek. This makes him blush and sit on the sofa, and his mum shoots a look at me that is something between a warning and a thank you.

'Right, both of you in the kitchen now and help me peel potatoes!' his mum says.

The kitchen's too small for all three of us so we grab everything and shift to the living room.

We get into this peel-fest in the living room, with buckets, potatoes, carrots and swedes. There's a game show on TV. Everyone gets involved.

'Rubbish!' shouts Marcus at the TV.

'Ask the audience, idiot!' goes his mum.

'It's B! B! B!' I shout.

The fool on the TV chooses A.

We all throw potato peel at him, even Leah.

His mum heads off into the kitchen, leaving us to watch the rest of the show. Leah's on Marcus's lap, playing with his hair. Just as the final credits roll, Marcus's dad blasts in, dumping two DJ bags on the floor and diving for the PC.

'Dad, Adele's stopping over tonight!' announces Marcus.

'Great,' says his dad, sticking a pen drive into the PC. 'Now listen to this track I just laid down. Catch the walking bass line. It's brill.'

'She'll be sleeping in Leah's room,' Marcus's mum tells her husband, coming into the living room.

'Excellent. Did she bring earplugs?'

'Marcus has lent me some PJs,' I say.

'That's very nice of him. Listen to this, Adele,' he says, like he's given up on his family and I'm the only one who will appreciate what he's done. 'This bass line, is it cool or is it cool?'

He plays some plodding music from Before Time. I smile and nod to it politely. Marcus kicks me and shakes his head, meaning, don't encourage him, but it's too late. His dad proceeds to play every track he's recorded, showing off his singing in styles ranging from a Cee Lo growl to a Sam Smith squeak, all of them out of tune. Thank God Marcus's mum puts a stop to it by saying everybody's got to sit at the table now, because tea's ready.

CHAPTER 15

HAVE A PLEASANT SLEEPY SLEEP, DARLINK

Eating at Marcus's is a unique experience. His dad wants us to eat while listening to *The Rivers of Babylon* because he likes the lead guitar riff and wants to sample it. His mum nixes that because she is trying to conduct an enquiry into who is stealing all the cooked sausages (neither of them is fessing up). There are big heaps of steaming chilli con carne and mashed potatoes on serving plates. Marcus is bored. He's shuffled off his shoes and is playing footsie with me under the table. I think he misdirects a foot and strokes his mum's leg because suddenly he yelps like his mum has whacked him under the table. He glowers at his mum, who smiles smugly with an I-told-you-so look. Leah copies Marcus's yelp, doing little baby yelps, which has everyone choking on the chilli con carne in laughter.

'This stuff's not hot enough,' declares Marcus's dad.

'Since when did you become an expert on chilli con carne?' says his mum.

'It's right up there in the name. It's "chilli con carne".

Chilli. With meat. Not "Meat with a hint of chilli". "Chilli. Con carne".

'Fair point,' says his mum. 'Coolio, here you go. Arriba.'

She unscrews the chilli shaker and sprinkles the equivalent of two spoonfuls of chilli over his plate.

She turns to me. 'How about you? Would you like an extra bit of chilli, Adele?'

'No thanks, Mrs Adenuga,' I say quickly.

'Call me Gillian. Or Mum. Marcus?'

'Nah, I'll leave it for now, Gillian,' says Marcus.

His mum cuts him a look.

His dad's on his own. He looks around at us. 'Chilli. ...Con carne,' he says, more hesitantly.

'Bueno. Bon apetita!' says his wife, waiting.

He looks at her. Then he looks over at Marcus. Marcus shrugs, in a you-dug-the-hole-Dad-so-you-climb-your-way-out-of-it way. His dad looks at me. I bite my lip so I don't smile. If there's anything on my face I'm hoping it's a Rather-You-Than-Me-But-I-Feel-Your-Pain-Mr-Adenuga look.

'OK,' he says. '.... But there's no rice!'

'There's potatoes,' Marcus's mum says.

'It's not the same.'

'It is the same.'

'Right.' Marcus's dad's fork wavers. He's waiting for intervention, divine or otherwise. None comes. Even Leah has stopped mushing her potatoes through her fingers and is looking at him.

Mr Adenuga gulps down four mouthfuls in a big rush. 'There,' he says, when he's done it. 'H'easy. H'Adele, Have you Had a Handsome Hour Horsing H'around with H'our Marcus? Heh?'

'It's been alright,' I reply.

'H'excellent. Here's Hoping you have Happy Hours Horsing H'all H'over H'England. Hoo. Hoo. Hoo.'

'Dad, you're talking nonsense. Drink some water.'

'So what did you two get up to today?' asks his mum.

'Nothing,' mutters Marcus.

'We went to a tattoo shop,' I say, 'but don't worry, we didn't get any tats.'

'It was down the road,' Marcus says. 'We didn't go into town. Before you ask.'

Leah starts to draw on her high chair tray, using potato as paint.

'Anybody want pudding?' Marcus's dad says. 'Ice cream. Any flavour so long as it's vanilla!' He rushes into the kitchen before anyone has a chance to answer.

After dinner we watch telly for a while. There's one long sofa and everyone's sprawled across it.

'I guess I've got to be getting Leah to bed,' Marcus's mum goes eventually. 'Can you run her bath please, Marcus?'

Marcus says nothing, like that makes him invisible to his mum so she won't ask him again. Leah is on my chest, her arms in my armpits, clinging to me. Her breathing's rock steady. 'I think she's asleep,' I say.

'Easy does it then,' says Mrs Adenuga and she slides her hands under her daughter and peels her off me. My chest is suddenly cold. Marcus nudges into me. His mum takes Leah upstairs. I guess Marcus's invisible cloak tactic worked.

Ten minutes later Mrs Adenuga is down again and taps me on the shoulder. 'OK, she's in her cot fast asleep, Adele. I've tried to put everything you might need on the bed but ask if there's anything else. You can take a shower if you want to but don't stay in it too long. I'm turning in soon and his dad has to do an early morning shift so...'

Marcus's dad nods. He's been very quiet and very still since we ate.

Mrs Adenuga's hinting it's time for me to go to bed. I'm amazed. It's only 10 o'clock. I get up. I do a little wave to Marcus. 'Nighty night,' I say to him. Marcus grunts by way of reply.

'Marcus!' his mum says, 'she's talking to you.'

'Goodnight, Adele, darlink, hope you have a pleasant sleepy sleep,' Marcus goes.

'That's better. Manners,' says his mum. Then, 'Goodnight Adele. After Adele, it's your dad, then you Marcus, then me. Chop chop, Adele. And remember, tiptoe. Don't wake Leah.'

No pressure then, I think. I ghost upstairs.

Leah's room is the smallest and it's next to the bathroom. I tip-toe in and glance into the cot. She is on her back, arms stretched out at eleven o'clock and one o'clock like she's directing a plane to fly above her. Marcus's mum's laid out a towel, soap and a toothbrush for me on the bed. I grab them, whizz to the bathroom, wet my head under the shower then climb into Marcus's onesie (it fits, just). I pad out of the bathroom onto the landing.

Marcus is at the top of the stairs.

I freeze, embarrassed.

160

'I wanted to see what you looked like in my PJs,' Marcus whispers to me, grinning from ear to ear.

'Marcus, get down here, right now!' his mum blasts from the foot of the stairs.

Marcus slinks down.

Has Marcus's mum's yell woken up the baby? I think, suddenly worried. I get to our bedroom door. It's quiet. I creep in. Leah's still flat on her back, arms at twelve o'clock and three o'clock, like she's now directing the plane to turn. I've crept back across the room and I'm just about to close our door when there's a rumble of stairs and Marcus's dad flies past.

'Sorry, love, gotta go!'

He hurtles into the bathroom and the toilet door bolt rattles.

I close Leah's room door as quietly as I can, creep across and climb into the fold-up bed. This bed's going to eat me, I'm sure, it's like some giant mouse trap. It's got a funny hinge right in the middle, and legs that wobble when you move so you have to be careful how you shift your weight. I test it, shifting my weight from one side to the other carefully. It makes creaking noises but it doesn't actually snap and trap me.

'Are you alright in there?'

It's Marcus's mum. At first I think she's asking me. But she's asking Marcus's dad who is still inside the bathroom. I've heard the toilet flush at least three times since he got in there.

'Get me some diarrhoea tablets, woman!' his dad groans.

I'm giggling in my mousetrap bed.

'Coming up,' says his mum. 'Authentic ones to help with your authentic chilli con carne.'

Mr Adenuga groans then farts.

It's a strange sleep-over, I think. I like the flowery smell of the quilt cover, the drifting cooking smells from downstairs and the baby talc smell. The poo smell isn't Leah, it's coming from the bathroom. I think he's still sat in there, on his chilli bum. What was Marcus up to on the landing when he saw me? I wonder if he is going to try come in here for a chat or a cuddle? He wouldn't dare would he, not with his mum on the alert – she's a dragon when she wants to be.

Everybody's in bed now. Leah's fast asleep. I think back to my shoplifting. What kind of crazy was that? It was good being able to say no to MC today, but if I hadn't been with Marcus, what would I have said? I bet she nicked loads today, she'll soon find a new recruit. I miss Mikaela, we're always arguing but she's like the sister I've never had, the one Mum was carrying then she lost her. Mum never talks about that but I wonder if it's why she's always drinking and drugging. I'm going to prove to Mum I can behave, I don't need to be stressing her anymore: she's stressed out enough as it is, and she doesn't even know what Dad's up to. My God, I'd forgotten about that. Nobody goes to bed this early in our house. My brother will have been wondering where I am, Mum will have told him, he'll have told Dad so there's either going to be an argument going on with things getting thrown, or maybe Dad will think I'm a runaway child, run off because I saw him on video snogging Mrs Robinson. That would be good. My dad is such a rat. He deserves some grief for that. Unless it was just an over-enthusiastic

162

kiss. Maybe Mikaela's mum wears invisible braces and Dad tripped and they got tangled so what was meant to be a quick peck on the cheek became a long snog because one of his lips was caught in her braces?

I'm jolted out of my dreaming by a strange whimper. I look around. It's Leah. Her mum's said if she cries I'm to keep totally still, don't move or say anything and she will go back to sleep. I hold my breath. The whimper sounds like it might go either way, become a mega-wail, or settle into nothing. I control my ribs, make sure they don't press on the iron bed frame and make any creaks. The whimper becomes a soft hiccup sound, then fades. Phew. I breathe easy again.

The football match was nuts. What a fuck up. Now I'm out of the England trials. Me and Mikaela really know how to mess things up. It was her stupid fault for starting the fight.

One of my feet is uncovered and starts throbbing with cold. I shift in the bed. The bed creaks.

There's a rumble from the cot. I glance up. Leah is standing, looking directly at me, like a prisoner behind bars. She isn't crying, just staring. We play statues for forty seconds. She wins, I have to move my foot, I can't help it. I move the foot and it sets her off on an ear-splitting screech. I watch, astonished, as she starts throwing a leg up at the cot's wooden side slats. On the third attempt she gets the foot hooked over the cot bar. She could topple over and smack her head on the floor any moment. I'm about to leap out of bed to catch her when she flops back onto her mattress. She does this hiccupy crying sound for a bit, then goes quiet. I daren't scratch my itchy foot. She's not sleeping. She's listening to me. I'm listening to her listen to me. It's a spy movie.

After ten minutes of this, I win and she's back asleep. I drift off. Suddenly I'm in a nightmare. I'm jumping off a cliff attached to a shoplifted bungee rope, plunging towards the water. I'm meant to bounce back up but Mikaela lets go of the rope and she's laughing as I plunge down in my monkey suit onesie. Dad's up on the cliff top snogging Mrs Robinson who's wearing fancy pink braces. Marcus has six legs and is playing keepy-uppy next to Mrs Robinson and my dad. I smack into the water. A thousand monkeys leap off the onesie and out of the water and I'm choking. The water becomes an arm, holding me down in the water, a hand pressing into my face. I'm gasping for air, suffocating. I heave myself out of the dream and prise my eyes open. I find Leah on top of me, her arm over my nose and mouth. How did she get here? She's asleep. She's asleep. She's definitely asleep. I ease my mouth free. I'm sure her mum will think I got her out of the cot. I'm thinking to carry her back to her cot, but she sniffles and opens one eye. I freeze. She closes the eye. I lift her arm to move her. She opens her eye again. I give up and lie back, her little arm pinning my neck to the mattress.

I'm exhausted and still sweating with fear from my dream. I stay as still as I can so Leah doesn't wake, and hold onto her so she doesn't fall out of the bed while she's strangling me in her sleep. I think I'm too scared of the dream coming back or Leah falling out of the bed to go back to sleep. I just lie there, looking at the ceiling.

CHAPTER 19

BREAKFAST IN A MONKEY ONESIE

Daylight is creeping through the Rupert Bear curtains. My toes are cold. Did I sleep? I don't think I ever got back to sleep at all. Whoever made up the saying 'to sleep like a baby' never slept with a baby. Suddenly I realise Leah is not on top of me. I panic. I look under the blanket. Not there. I look around the bed. Not there. I scramble up and look in the cot. Not there. Under the cot. No. Under the bed. Not there either. I'm close to crying. The bedroom door is a teeny bit open. Maybe she got out. Maybe she's crawled out and fallen down the stairs. *Ohmygod I've killed Leah.* I dash to the door. She's not on the landing. I rush down the stairs. Not at the bottom of the stairs. I can hear voices. I go into the living room.

Marcus's mum is there. Leah is in her arms.

'Did you have a nice sleep?' Mrs Adenuga asks.

'Leah climbed out of the cot!' I blurt.

Marcus is on the sofa. He laughs. 'Nooo. You picked her up, didn't you? Ha ha ha. Bet you was stuck with her kicking and fighting you round the bed all night!'

'She climbed out,' I protest to Mrs Adenuga.

'Calm down, I believe you. Adele. I knew she would. "Any day soon", I said to her father. She's at that stage. It's not your fault, Adele. Did you have her a long time? No wonder you look a bit bleary-eyed.'

'I was scared she'd do it again and hurt herself so...'

'She was happy as Larry in your arms, Adele. I took her off you this morning to give you a bit of rest.'

I look at Leah. She's fresh as a button and gurgling away in a crisp new baby suit. She reaches for my hair. I let her pull it.

'You picked her up out of the cot!' insists Marcus.

'Marcus stop it!' says his mum. Then to me: 'He always gets up with a sore head, don't pay him no mind, Adele. I'm going to make you some breakfast then you've got to head back home, I promised your mum.'

Marcus is staring at me weirdly. Suddenly I realise I'm in his monkey onesie and I look ridiculous. I back out of the room using my hands to cover myself up as best I can.

'You want to take my PJs home with you?' sniggers Marcus. 'They look better on you than me!'

I give him the finger, finish backing out of the room, and dash upstairs to change.

CHAPTER 20

THE AMBUSH

It's hard to watch the tears slide down the face of your best friend and drip onto her school tie. Yet I don't feel like trying to stop her from crying, so I wait in the chair next to her. The classroom has emptied; it's just me and her. Eventually, she has her final sniffle then asks. 'What do we do?'

Mikaela's convinced my dad and her mum are having an affair. She won't let it rest.

'You're the brainy one,' I say to her, 'you tell me.'

There is a silence between us and I see her brain go to work. It's one of the things I love about Mikaela. She frowns, her nose squints and wrinkles, then her eyebrows play tag across her forehead as ideas get tossed from side to side. When her lips pull back and the tip of her tongue peeps out, I know she's got something.

'What?' I ask her.

'I have the coordinates of where they meet,' she says. 'I checked my mum's satnav app and she goes to the same place, same time every Friday lunchtime. Broadway Cinema. I know it's them because Mum's tagged the destination with "Vincent". That's your dad's name, isn't it?'

'Friday's today.'

'We can ambush them.'

'Genius.'

'I'm scared though, Adele, there was other stuff on her phone.'

'Like porno?'

'"I daydream about you all the time". "I feel your pain deep in my heart". "I want to hold you in my arms and feed you Belgian chocolates".'

'From my dad?'

She nods.

'Yuk.'

I start imagining my dad in Mikaela's mum's arms but it's hard because in my imagination my dad always looks stiff in anybody's arms, he doesn't do relaxation. I try to imagine them sitting on a sofa, back to back, leaning into each other and it works better like that. They could even feed each other Belgian chocolate from that position, with a bit of twisting and turning.

Suddenly I think, *what about my mum?* How will she feel if all this is going on?

'This isn't happening,' I tell Mikaela.

Mikaela's frown deepens. 'If they get married I'm not going to the wedding and if the vicar says does anyone object, I'll object. They do ask. It's not just in films, right?'

I'm listening to the thump of my heart. 'We could end up living together,' I tell her, 'and having to share a room. I'd kill you. I've seen you, Mikaela. Even in class, you start organising things in rows. I'd stab you before I let you organise my clothes.'

'I'd have stabbed you first,' Mikaela says.

I turn my head away. When I turn back, she's brushing tears off her face again. 'This is so fucked up,' she says. She stands up and shoves her chair back. 'Let's catch them.'

We sneak out at lunchtime and catch a bus to Broadway Cinema.

The white tipped tail of a black cat is twitching slowly to and fro, under a car in the car park. We're by the Pure Gym swimming pool fire exit doors. The smell of chlorine mixes with car fumes. I've pulled my coat hood up and the fake fur trim sticks in my face. Mikaela is chewing gum. She never chews gum. I want a wee. We've been waiting ages.

'I'm going to count to ten. If we don't see them by then, they're not coming,' says Mikaela.

'Shut up,' I tell her.

There's CCTV covering us but there's other kids around. There must be a secondary school nearby that's let them out for lunch.

The car park cat leaps at a tree trunk and a bird rushes out of its branches. At the same time, I spot Dad's black car parked in the furthest away part of the car park. How did I not spot it before? I nudge Mikaela and point to the car. Mikaela gasps then calls to the cat *kitty kitty kitty* and clicks her tongue at it. I stop her.

Holding hands, we go along the raised narrow path between two rows of parked cars. The path runs out as we get further out into the car park. Mikaela bumps along behind me in her chunky school shoes.

I tell myself it will be OK, if they're both in the car it's because they are probably working on a project together.

Mikaela is struggling to keep up and I'm practically

dragging her along. There is a wide open zone of tarmac between us and Dad's car. The stupid cat has followed Mikaela. I shoo it away. Arms linked, we walk the last twenty metres of no-man's land and reach the car. There's no one in the front seats. Mikaela is about to tap on a darkened window at the back. I tug her round to the driver's window and we look through.

Dad has a hand on Mikaela's mum's chest and he's kind of clambered over her, kissing her.

'Get off my mum, you pig!' Mikaela screams, kicking the car.

Mikaela grabs the handle of the back door. It's locked. She bashes its window with her shoe. My dad has looked up, startled. He sees her. He sees me. Mikaela's still banging on the window.

The two of them sit up and start fixing buttons and pulling clothes straight. They're out of the car almost as fast as their excuses.

'Adele, I can explain! Stop kicking me!'

'Dad, what are you doing?'

'We were just fooling around! Stop it!'

'Fool with this, then!'

'Mikaela, leave him be!' Mrs Robinson shouts.

Mikaela has swung a kick at my dad. He jumps out of the way and her shoe goes flying. She takes the other one off and swings that at him but misses, trips and falls.

Mrs Robinson leans over to help Mikaela up but she yells, 'piss off!' at her mum.

'Mrs Robinson, I'm so sorry,' Dad says. He has his hand on her again.

170

'You're a racist, Dad, remember?' I yell at him. 'That means you can't be going out with a black woman!'

'Watch your mouth, girl,' Mrs Robinson say to me. Then to Dad, 'why does she say that?'

Dad shrugs and mutters 'Kids!' like that explains it all.

Mrs Robinson grabs a briefcase from the back seat. 'I have a meeting,' she says. She walks off, with Mikaela trailing behind her shouting at her back and trying to pull her shoes back on at the same time.

It's just me and Dad now. Dad sighs and smoothes his shirt and trousers.

'Don't go making more of this than-'

'Dad, don't push me.' I say. I turn and walk away. I can hear him calling me, with his "I-can-explain-everything" voice. I think, *that works on Mum, Dad, but it doesn't work on me.*

This time he doesn't chase after me.

I meet up with Mikaela an hour later at the Dallas Chicken Shop. We share a £1.99 chicken meal. She tells me her mum was so ashamed and apologised.

'My mum was all, "I'll make it up to you, I'm really sorry, I was tired and foolish."'

'My dad doesn't do shame,' I say.

'Do you think they'll stop seeing each other?' Mikaela's still stunned.

'Only if he has to. My dad never gives anything up unless he has to. He's a narcissist.'

'He takes drugs?'

'He fancies himself,' I explain.

'Oh, I get it. Like Sleeping Beauty.'

'You've lost me, Mikay.'

'"Mirror, mirror, on the wall, who's the most beautiful of them all? Me!" Sleeping Beauty.'

Sometimes Mikaela talks stuff that is way above my head. I nod at her then say, 'Do you like the new spicy wings dip?'

Mikaela doesn't hear me. 'It's all excuses.'

I agree. 'Adults are good at excuses.'

'She said my dad never loved me, I was a trap for him, but I don't believe her, she's just lawyering. I don't know why my dad sticks with her.'

'Will you tell him?' I ask. Really, I'm thinking about my mum - do I tell her?

'She asked me to keep it a secret.'

'Secrets suck,' I say. 'My dad's had loads of affairs. Your mum's just the latest one.'

Mikaela looks at me like I've scraped my football studs right along her shin. She starts sobbing.

I eat her spicy chicken wings for her.

We spend hours just wandering around Broadway.

It gets dark and eventually we split and I go home. Dad's car is not on the driveway. I open the front door. The black swan is in three pieces on the hallway floor.

Inside the lounge, the coffee table is upturned and the flower picture is off the wall, its frame glass smashed across the marble floor. There's a smear of blood on the floor, then drips.

I follow the drips into the kitchen. Knives, forks, spoons are scattered about. Blood is on a sink tap handle and along the stem of the mixer tap. There's a diamond earring at the back of the sink, by the tap. *Mum's.*

I need to get to Mum's room fast.

I run straight into my brother. He's in the lounge, looking lost.

'Where've you been?' he asks.

'Did Dad hit Mum?'

He looks at all the mess like it's the first time he's noticed it. Then he says, 'You did this.'

'Duh. I wasn't here, remember?'

'Dad went nuts. Called you a snitchy, spoilt brat. Or was it "spoilt, snitchy brat"? I can't remember. What's that about?'

'Fuck off, Anthony.'

'He said you could have been the poster girl of the World Cup for Girls campaign.'

'Like I care.'

'He'd arranged it all. You. Fucked. It. Up. Well done, little sister, it takes someone special to fuck that up.'

I punch him in the chest. He traps my hands. I say, 'where's Mum?' When he still doesn't answer, I pull away from him and take the stairs. He follows me, saying stuff, but I'm not listening. The staircase bounces up and down.

Mum's at the top of the stairs.

She looks like an extra out of a Zombie movie. One eye is swollen and there's bits of dried blood all over her face. She keeps her hands in her face as she's talking. 'That's enough you two,' she groans. 'I need to talk to both of you.'

She turns and drags her feet back to her room. We follow obediently.

Dad's not in the room. Mum pats the bed. I sit next to her. MTB sits on the floor at her feet.

'Tony, you must stop teasing your sister like that. She has temper issues,' Mum says, 'Your teasing her doesn't help.'

'I do not have temper issues,' I tell Mum. She ignores me.

'Sorry,' MTB says meekly to Mum. He blows me a silent raspberry as Mum moves a pillow to prop herself up with.

'Mum?' I say, fingering the bruise on her cheekbone.

She traces the bruise with me. 'It was the kitchen cupboard. When I get drunk, I bang my head on things.' She shifts her pillows again. 'Tony, what happened between me and your father had nothing to do with your sister's sponsorship thing. That wasn't ... that didn't ... that isn't ...'

Mum's shaking her head side to side. She opens her eyes again as I pat her hand. 'The thing is...' She swallows. 'Your dad's having an affair.'

MTB cuts Mum's tears off. 'Again?' he says, sarcastically.

I'm thinking, *so Mum knows about Dad's affair.* I suppose that's good. I look suitably shocked. 'Who with?' I ask.

'What does it matter who with?' snaps Mum.

Now I know that Mum does not know that it's with my best friend's mum.

'He admitted it,' Mum continues, 'so we had a discussion and we agreed that him moving out was the sensible thing to do.'

'C'mon, Mum,' MTB cuts in. 'You had a blazing row, he admitted he'd been shagging this Bimbo for the last two months. You asked for his phone to check, he wouldn't give it you so you chucked your wedding ring at him, he threw the swan at you and you threw the picture at him.

You called him boring and he called you ugly and struck you across the face. Then he stormed out.'

'Tony, I've told you before not to eavesdrop on your father and my conversations.'

'It was ninety decibels, Mum. They heard you in France.'

'Anyway,' Mum says, 'what happened's happened. There's no going back... I can't find my medication. Did I take it already? Have you both done your homework? Your uniforms ... Adele, you've got split ends, dear.'

She has been examining my hair as she says all this. MTB's eyes flick with worry at me because Mum's rambling. I shake my head to him to say 'don't worry'. He kisses Mum, almost on the bruise. She strokes his hand. Then it's just me and Mum.

'Did you have a nice time at ... at ... at ...?' asks Mum.

I'm impressed she remembers.

I nod.

'I'm sorry, I'm really sorry, Adele, about what I said. I didn't mean it.'

She sniffs my hair and lets out a little sob.

'It's OK, Mum. Do you need your medicine?'

'I ... I think I took it already.'

'Water?'

She strokes my face. 'You so look like your dad at times. I wonder where he's gone,' she says.

'Don't let Dad get away with it this time,' I tell her, 'Anthony's right, he's done it too often.'

For a brief moment Mum's face hardens. 'I told him to go be with his frigging fancy woman!' she spits. Then her anger fades and something like fear takes over. 'She'll be pretty,' Mum says, 'very pretty... He'll have booked into a hotel. He's had work pressures. Something about Turkey. I think he might be having a breakdown actually. I hope he's alright. He used to compliment me. ... I do have crows' feet around my eyes ... I need Botox. And a boob job.'

'Stop it, Mum, you're not ugly. And Dad *is* boring.'

'He wasn't always boring, Adele. We used to go to parties together. He'd dance so wild and beautiful. Expressive. Everyone would be in a circle, cheering him on. He was hot then. We were the hot couple. Nobody did the clubs the way me and your dad did the clubs... Back then they played music you could dance to. Disco music.'

Mum gets up and starts to dance in the room. It's more Middle East dancing than disco, but that's because of the drugs, I guess. I take her hands and we dance like this. It's the first time we've danced together in ages and it feels good, even though she's off her head and will never remember it.

'I was a rock chick,' Mum mumbles. 'A dancer in a nightclub. I was paid to dance. I danced and other people came on and danced and filled the floor ... I got the party going. It's how I met your dad.'

'Show me your moves, Mum.'

'I will one day, just you wait. It was none of this booty-shaking you do nowadays. It was all in the hands and the footwork.'

Mum tries a fancy move, I think it was meant to be a spin, but she stumbles. I steady her, guide her back to the bed and prop her back up with pillows. She waves away the water I offer her. 'I was good you know. A very sexy dancer.'

'Of course you were, Mum.'

176

'I was ...' She starts a tuneful mumbling, making up nonsense lyrics. "'Disco queen ... see a thousand me's spinning in that disco ball ... "See that girl ... she could dance..."'

As Mum half-talks, half-sings, her eyes get hazier and hazier until she slides off the stack of pillows and falls asleep.

I pull a cover over her then tiptoe out. MTB's got his music blasting. When I get downstairs, I put the coffee table back together again and sweep up the flower picture glass. In the kitchen, I find whiskey behind the fridge and pour it down the sink. I decide to hide the empty bottle in the drum of the old washing machine in the garage but when I open the drum door, I find another half full bottle so I tip that down the sink too, then hide both bottles in the old plastic picnic box instead. I turn off all the lights.

Next morning, there's still no sign of Dad. I make some tea and take it to Mum on a tray with toast, bacon and eggs. MTB gallops past me. I've left him enough breakfast to keep him happy. I help Mum sit up, and as she pecks at the scrambled eggs (and moans, "why is it not still night-time?") I climb onto the bed and sit behind her, brushing her hair.

'Is the bacon crispy enough, Mummy?' I ask, as I coax a brush through her hair.

'The bacon's adorable, darling. Did Marcus snore?' she asks, her canny-parent eyebrows flicking upwards at me.

'I don't know Mum, because I slept in Leah's room. With the baby ... She got out of the cot and slept with me.'

Mum goes quiet. Babies is a painful subject for her. Ever since she lost my sister. I keep on stroking her hair. I decide I'm going to plait it, French style. 'My sister would have been eleven now, wouldn't she, Mum?'

'Eleven and three months,' Mum says.

'You could have been plaiting her hair while I plait yours,' I say. 'Putting those silver bobbles in what you used to put in mine, remember?'

A circle of water appears on one of Mum's thumbs.

'She had big locks of hair,' Mum says. 'Curlier than yours. Like candyfloss. Your dad's hair ... She was beautiful. We never got to know her. It hurts your dad. Sometimes he cries in his sleep. He wants another child. To replace Cara. I can't give him one, I think that's why he...'

'No, Mum,' I say. 'He has affairs because he's a cheating bastard!'

'Adele! He's your father.'

'So?' I've half plaited her hair. I stop. 'Do you like it?'

'Very chic,' Mum says, looking across to her dressing room mirror.

'You've said worse about him.'

'But he's my husband. That's different.'

'Is he good for you though, Mum?'

Mum does one of her avoiding-the-question answers. 'We may have to sell the house. I don't know if the loan companies own it all now, I haven't seen the papers...'

She witters on as I finish plaiting her hair.

I'm on edge all day, listening out for the sound of tyres on gravel, but Dad does not come back.

At night I can't sleep. Thoughts tumble around in the

178

giant washing machine of my head. What is my dad up to? Has he really left Mum? Is he with Mrs Robinson? Are they going to go on holiday together? Is Mikaela to be his step-daughter now? Will he tell off Mikaela, choose her A-levels and stuff, like Dads do? But that doesn't make sense because Mikaela's dad's come back, she said. Does Mikaela have two dads now? Or maybe her dad came back and then left again? Is it my fault Mum and Dad have split? If I didn't give Mum such a hard time, she wouldn't be so alcoholic then she would pay more attention to Dad and he wouldn't need go off with Mrs Robinson to get some attention. What if his car crashes into a river, with me and Mikaela in it and we're both drowning? Who would he pull out first? Me? Mikaela? Why does he even like Mrs Robinson when he's a racist? Is it like the thing we say we hate the most, secretly we love? What if Mikaela's mum gets pregnant by Dad? Me and Mikaela would be related then. Does Dad really want another baby to replace my dead sister? Will Mikaela be seeing more of my dad than me? Will her mum start choosing my dad's clothes? Where will he spend Christmas? Does Mum still get all Dad's money if he dies? Will Mum leave and Dad come back and move Mikaela's mum in, then me and Mikaela would be living together, maybe even sharing my room? Do I need to kill Mikaela to stop all of this?

It's all so brain-aching. My head goes numb. I try to sleep. All I get is nightmares.

CHAPTER 21

MUM'S BUCKET LIST

It's half term. We haven't heard from Dad for forty-eight hours. Mum's feeling it. I tell her forget him, what does she want to do with her life?

We're having a fried egg on granary bread lunch. Mum makes a bucket list:

Mum's Bucket List:

☑ Get fit

☑ Someone to wander round town shopping with

☑ Someone to see a Musical with

☑ Visit to Milan Fashion Week

☑ Dance with a Hollywood star

☑ See the Aurora Borealis (Northern Lights)

We're munching on the granary bread when the bell goes. It's not Dad, it's the pharmacist van. He drives up and delivers Mum a package. Mum's eyes get all excited. I'm about to tell her off when she shushes me, hands me one of the boxes and tells me to read it.

The drug has a name I can't pronounce but which ends in *iram*. The instructions say it is a treatment against drinking and 'reacts to ingestion of alcohol'.

'Huh?'

'If I drink, it makes me throw up,' Mum explains.

'So it will cure you?'

'Nothing's ever that simple, but yes.'

She takes a tablet with a swig of orange juice. We both wait a while to see if she drops dead, which she doesn't. Or throws up. Which she doesn't. Or starts hallucinating. Which she also doesn't. I'm proud of her. Mum moves around the kitchen putting things away. Dad's left but she's holding her head up high and getting on with her life. I notice her hair is going a bit grey at the back. She's a bit young to be going grey already. I hope it isn't hereditary.

'Mum, can we visit Cara?'

Mum whips round. 'Why do you say that?'

'I miss her sometimes. Don't you?'

Mum goes into a flood of tears.

I wait till she's settled. 'Come on, Mum, it will be good for you.'

'But I can't just turn up, I don't feel it's the right time, I...'

'You can. It is. Get changed then let's go.'

Mum moans but in the end she agrees.

CHAPTER 22

CONFRONTING GHOSTS

A two mile drive later, me and Mum are in a graveyard. It's a sunny afternoon. Mum has stuffed her face with pharmacy drugs. She's dressed like she's going to a cocktail bar – a blinged black and gold top, flapper trousers, white kid leather gloves, black Stilettos and a little black pill box hat. I'm wearing my ordinary clothes. My little sister will have to take me as I am.

I've not been to a graveyard before and I keep my head down because when I look up all I see is about six football pitches of gravestones. I can't get rid of this thought that among them there might be somebody who they've buried alive and maybe they're trying to call out to me, or they've got a little bell in their coffin and they're ringing it like mad trying to alert me.

I take a deep breath and keep walking.

Maybe they were right to keep me from my little sister's funeral. All I remember of the day is Mum scrubbing me in the bath hard, lots of people I didn't know rushing from room to room crying, others in corners talking in whispers, the cat chasing up the fireplace and staying there, Dad shouting about who has to ride in which car, Mum wanting the flowers in the coffin car rearranged, Dad's mum squeezing my cheek and kissing me, rubbing her nose into mine and me thinking we look so alike, Mia the maid scooping me up as I screamed because I wanted to go to where my sister sleeping in the box was going.

I follow Mum's heels. She goes through the gravestones, lurching like a drunken slalom skier. Finally she stops by a beautiful, polished white headstone. She crosses herself, even though she's not a Catholic, then falls to her knees and after a bit of wailing starts on a speech with lots of Angels and Forgives and Big Sister's Here Too and If Onlys in it. I'm not listening because I've heard it all before when Mum's drunk. Instead, I read the writing on the headstone. It's then I realise it's not even my sister's grave.

'Mum,' I say, interrupting her and pointing to the name chipped into the stone. Mum clears her eyes carefully so she doesn't brush her contact lenses out. 'Oh God,' she mutters. She gets up and starts off in a new direction. She makes bee-lines from place to place but none of her guesses are right. I start thinking maybe we're not even in the right cemetery.

'Mum, you don't know where she is, do you?'

I taste glove fibres on my lips as Mum's smacked me across the face. She gasps and falls to the ground, pulling at my trousers. 'What have I done to deserve this? Oh, God.' This carries on for a while.

Two men are standing by a pile of earth and some wooden boards. They say something to each other then one of them leans off his spade and comes clumping over to us. Mum's not seen him so when he taps her on the shoulder she startles. He's got a crinkly old face and listens patiently as Mum gets up and babbles twenty kinds of nonsense up his nose. Somehow he manages to get what he needs out of her. He lets her place an arm on his shoulder and leads her, slowly because her heels are sinking every step, across the graveyard. He counts headstone rows silently with little nods of his head, then cuts into a row, walks along and points. It's a small white headstone. It has my sister's name on it.

Mum stands frozen, staring. I lift my head up and manage a smile at the gravedigger. He looks back at me with steady eyes. I think, *if only I had him for a mum or a dad.*

As soon as the gravedigger has turned his back, Mum steals some fluffy toys off nearby graves and arranges them on my sister's plot. She gets the little white plastic fence that goes round the grave upright then pulls a few weeds out that are growing through the white chip stones. She uses her hankie to clean the headstone. As she cleans, her wailing starts up again.

'I know you are on God's knee and he's brushing your hair, you are one of his best angels. When I gazed into your eyes before you left I saw how graceful you were, you were going to be brilliant at school and look after your mum so well, you were going to be perfect, a mother's dream. My angel, you would have been appalled at what your big sister gets up to. She would behave so much better if you'd been around, she'd have had to be an example. And your father would never have strayed, he would have kissed my hands every night, worshipped me as Mother Mary.

You would have had all the best tings, I already had the Gabbana bootees, I would have been so proud showing you off. Everyone would have wanted a curl off your beautiful hair, your little toes were perfect, so was your little nose...'

I tune out of Mum's babble and whisper, 'sleep well' to my sister, then watch from the path as Mum talks on. She's got her arms around the headstone now. I'm worried she's trying to pull it up and take it with us. About fifteen minutes pass before Mum finishes.

She makes it back to the cemetery path, eyes streaming, and says, 'I feel better now.' Her hands are shaking, which I take to be the drugs kicking in more. When we get to the car, she passes me the key.

'Drive, Adele, please.'

'Mum–'

'Don't play innocent with me, Adele. I've seen you take your dad's car up and down the drive, you can drive this little thing.'

Handbrake. Neutral. Ignition. I move the car off. It lurches and Mum complains. She has the vanity mirror down on the passenger side and is redoing her lip stick. She settles back as I pull out of the cemetery. 'I'm going to do this every Anniversary,' she says. She keeps on. 'Sometimes I see her on the back seat and I say, "put your seat belt on, Cara, silly girl".' Mum dabs her eyes.

It's a miracle, but I get us home.

CHAPTER 23

HALF TERM MATCH

Even though it's half term, we've got a football match at school which is crazy because everyone goes on holiday abroad at half term. I phone and text Mikaela but she's not answering. I find out from other girls that she's fed up and not playing. I decide to play. Mum begs to come. I allow her but tell her it's my rules so she can't run on the pitch, she can't do any crazy arm pumping, and she has to pass an alcohol test before she can even stand on the touchline. She accepts all terms.

We get there a bit late so I dash out of the car into the changing rooms and get changed fast. When I make it onto the pitch, Mum is on the touchline. I run up to her.

'Mum.'

'What?'

'Breathe in my face.'

'Must I?'

I nod.

While she breathes on me, I smell. It's a mix of spicy sausage, cat breath, sour milk and brown sugar.

'Do I pass?' she asks.

'Yes. Have a mint, though.'

The match starts.

Whenever I glance across, Mum is standing looking

chilled, nodding. Not jumping up and down, not cursing, and not invading the pitch. Just once she can't contain herself and calls out:

'Get on Goal Attack, Dell, stick to her like Velcro!'

I let the yell slide. But when we start scoring goals, Mum starts doing some disco moves. I dash over before I die of embarrassment.

'No more disco, OK?'

Mum nods and folds her arms again. 'We're cool,' she says.

She spends the rest of the match standing on one spot, arms folded, nodding. Perfect.

We win. I mark Mum's Report Card. Very good. Keep It Up.

Four Things That Turn Brown

☺ CHEESE ON TOAST — AT THE TOP AND EDGES

☺ TONSILS WHEN YOU EAT CHOCOLATE

☺ MY SKIN AFTER FOUR WEEKS IN THE SUN

☺ MY MUM'S HAIR WHEN SHE DYES IT

CHAPTER 24

DEALING WITH STUFF*

Yes, she is curled up in a sad ball.

Yes, she's got so many lines on her face you could write the lyrics to Beyoncé's entire back catalogue on them.

Yes, it is going to give her a shock.

No, I feel no pity.

I press the button. A death metal wail comes screeching out at 160 watts per channel, zooming out of my iPod into Mum's bedroom's surround sound speakers.

Mum pushes the quilt back, rubs her eyes, sticks her tongue out to taste the air, focuses. Then shouts at me. 'Adele, I'll kill you! Turn that off!' She throws a slipper at me.

Mission accomplished. She is out of bed and it is not even 9am.

'What's this?' she groans as she pulls on her dressing gown

I have done a trail of leaves on her floor. 'Follow them, Mum,' I say.

Rubbing her eyes, she places foot after foot and the leaves take her into the shower. 'You now have five minutes to take your shower,' I tell her.

'May I take my nightie off first?'

'You may. I'll have breakfast waiting for us downstairs.'

After breakfast, we get changed into our jogging gear for a jog along the riverside trail. At least that was the plan. At the last minute, Mum worries the neighbours will see her without make-up.

I tell her they'd need high powered binoculars and it's just excuses. We do a deal: we will start with walking and then move into jogging.

As we walk, Mum stops to listen to the birds. Then to the rustle of leaves in the willow trees. Then to see dogs chasing down to the river's edge barking at ducks. We do two minutes of jogging but Mum starts panting and goes all giddy, so we do a warm down walk home. We finish with a sprint to the front door which I win easily.

While Mum tries to drink the tap dry, I get us two Vitamin Waters from the fridge. She drinks one off then goes to answer the call of nature.

'Ugh! Ugh! Ugh!'

Mum's run back the kitchen, dry heaving.

'What's the matter?' I ask her.

'The toilet's blocked. Disgusting. Call your dad.'

'We can unblock it ourselves.'

'I'm as feminist as the next woman,' Mum says, while trying to breathe only through her mouth so she doesn't smell anything, 'but if men want to show off their muscles by unblocking toilets we should leave them to it.'

'How does Dad do it?'

'He gets a stick with this rubbery pink cup thing on the end of it, then shoves it in and pulls.'

189

'OK. Let's find that rubbery pink stick thing. It'll be in the garage.'

'A plunger.'

'Rubbery pink stick thing sounds more fun.'

Before you know it, we're both peering into the toilet bowl at you-know-what. It's full to the brim. 'Whose is it?' I ask.

'Anthony's of course.'

I think, yeh, that sounds right, he's full of it. I have the plunger in my hand. 'What part of this needs a man on the end of it?'

'You do it then,' Mum says. She's backing away.

For a nanosecond I wonder how she ever managed to wipe my bum as a baby if she backs away this much from stuff. 'We'll do it together. You put a hand on it, then me.'

Craftily, Mum places her hand on the top part of the stick so my hand has to go lower and nearer the stuff*. We plunge. There is a lot of rubbery wobble wibble sounds then a throaty gurgle sound and stuff bubbles away in the toilet bowl. It looks like it's all going down but suddenly it comes back up and explodes on us. We're covered in stuff.

Mum's too stunned to scream. I look at her then avoid looking in the bathroom mirror in case I look like Mum. I look down. The toilet has partly cleared. Mum hits the toilet flush button. Water disappears in a torrent the way it should, taking the rest of the brown stuff with it.

'We did it,' Mum declares, holding my dirty, plunging hand up. 'We dealt with stuff!' Then she starts gagging again at the sight of the stuff on me and dives for the shower room.

*FOR PUBLISHING REASONS, THE WORD 'STUFF' HAS BEEN USED THROUGHOUT THIS CHAPTER WHEN ANOTHER WORD MIGHT COME INTO YOUR MIND. YES. THAT. APPARENTLY, OCCASIONAL USE OF THE WORD 'STUFF' IS PERMISSIBLE WITH A CHAPTER, BUT TOO MUCH 'STUFF' IN ONE CHAPTER IS NOT.

CHAPTER 25

THE BIG WHEEL

Once we're both showered and changed, we go into town to tick off item one on her bucket list. Deansgate Central is the swankiest part of town, though it wouldn't matter to me if we were strolling through the fish market. We are arm in arm; she's wearing her Versace dress that she last wore three years ago at one of Dad's work's parties, I'm wearing a plain black A-line dress and Mum's pearls because she let me. Oh, and my Nike trainers. I look at people as we stroll. If money brings happiness, the people here should be rolling on the pavement laughing all day. Instead, they look nervously around or stare intensely into shop windows. I like the warmth of Mum's arm in mine, how we can match strides. We get some admiring glances from men. Mum's astonished when some of them actually look me over as well as her and she asks how long has that been going on. I say it's even worse when I'm in uniform, believe it or not. She holds onto me tighter and asks how is Marcus my boyfriend and whether that was who I was texting in the car and why am I so secretive about him, she doesn't mind if I have a boyfriend so long as we don't do anything (meaning have sex) as I'm too young for that. I say Marcus was telling me he's about to play a match and should he change studs because the grass is wet? Mum's not listening to me now though, she's spotted something. She drags me to a window and gazes at diamond bracelets.

She has no money. She did have a credit card of Dad's but couldn't remember the PIN number for it and the cash machine snaffled it.

'Your father knows I've got no money. How he expects me to...' She bites her tongue.

In the end she goes next door to buy a hat. I say I can't stand hats and I'll meet her outside. Little does she know, I have one of Dad's credit cards. I nip back into the jewellers.

When Mum comes out, she's wearing what looks like a plain hat to me but she says it's modelled on the Queen's. We go to the Slow River restaurant to celebrate, Mum walking all the way there as royally as possible.

As we're sat at the restaurant, through the plate glass window I notice the Big Wheel. It's all lit up and the glass gondolas go round and round taking you high into the sky. 'Mum, let's do the Wheel, me and you, please!' I say.

Mum does a royal frown. 'We don't like heights.'

'Oh, I'll give you all my Kingdom, all my jewels and every pear on my pear tree if you go on it with me.'

Mum softens. 'We shall consider it,' she says. 'Let us process that way.'

Five minutes later, we're at the entrance.

'In you get!' the Big Wheel loading guy says.

Mum hesitates. She hasn't realised the gondola floor itself is glass as well as the sides.

'It's rock solid,' the guy assures her. He's wearing a smart black T shirt with a Big Wheel logo on it, and he swishes his pony tail like fairground Wurlitzer guys do.

Mum backs away.

I get in. 'Look, it's perfectly safe,' I say. I start wiggling around, then do a pogo dance to show her the floor is solid. I end up by doing a complete dance routine. The Big Wheel guy's eyes bulge. I smooth my dress down.

'See there, safe as houses,' he says to Mum.

Reluctantly, Mum steps forward. 'Shoes off,' he says to her.

'Why?' Mum asks.

'Stilettos. Like pick axes. Can shatter the glass.'

'I thought you said it was rock solid?'

'It is. A pick axe can break rock. But don't worry love, I'll catch you in my arms if you fall.' He leers at her.

'We are not amused,' Mum says. She sheds her shoes and steps in. He closes the gondola door.

'The things I do for you,' Mum says to me. The gondola lurches forwards and up.

'That's why I love you and you're the best mum in the world ever,' I say quickly, so she doesn't notice the lurching. I hold onto her tight.

As we start rising higher and higher, Mum looks at me intently. She definitely does not look anywhere else.

'Come on, Mum, look out, that's where all the fun is.'

'Stop moving around, Adele, you're making me dizzy.'

'I'm not moving, Mum.'

We're almost at full height. She's closed her eyes. I look around. 'I'll describe it for you since you don't want to look yourself. We're above all the department stores. You can still see all the silver jewellery twinkling. There's a gym on the top floor of the building close to us and lots of sweaty people on exercise bikes looking bored. The tops of the buildings all have big metal tubes zigzagging across them. Over there's where Marcus lives.'

'Where?'

The Wheel has stopped and we're at the top. Finally she's looking. I point out the zone where Marcus lives.

She scowls. 'That's a council estate.'

'And?'

'It's very pretty. From up here. Now can you please ask him to get us down, I'm feeling unwell.'

The Wheel jerks to life, goes a little lower but stops five seconds later.

Mum curses. 'What is wrong with this thing? Why has he stopped it? Is it broken?' She's peering at the tiny control box at ground level.

'Mum well done, you just looked down.'

'Did I? Yes, I did.' She sits back, chuffed with herself. 'Once is enough though. Tell him to take us down, right now.'

She seems to think I have a hotline to Mr Gondola-PonyTail-Wurtlitzer. I get out my phone and pretend to be texting him. Then I say, 'Smile, Mum!' She lashes out at me to try stop me but I take her pic. It's great. I show it to her. 'Budge over,' I say. We take a selfie together. This all distracts her from the height. There are seven more lurches of the Wheel as they let people out of the gondolas before us, before our own gondola door slides open. Mum staggers out and pulls her shoes on. 'Never again,' she says.

She clings to me as we walk away from the Wheel.

When we get home I give her the bracelet she liked.

'Did you...?' she asks, ready to be angry.

'No I did not rob it. I used one of Dad's credit cards. I wanted to surprise you.' I hand her the card and tell her the PIN number.

'Oh, you gorgeous thing,' says Mum, looking from the bracelet to the credit card, but mostly at the credit card.

In the evening, we talk films. Mum says she thought she had a significant role in Dad's life but it turned out she only had a walk-on part; still, she's ready for the spotlight again.

CHAPTER 26

FEVER, BOLEROS & CEILINGS

Half term just gets better and better. Mum booked tickets for Saturday Night Fever the Musical using the credit card. When MTB found out, he wanted her to change the tickets to the Rocky Horror Show but Mum refused. 'Sorry. Girls Night Out!' she told him. Ha. Ha.

We're in Mum's bedroom and she's getting glammed up. She's dug out a pair of platform shoes and a white suit. She's going as the Saturday Night Fever hero himself, Tony Moreno. She sings "Dancing Queeeeen!" in the shower. She comes out and says, 'You lookin at me? You lookin at me?'

I tell her she's got her films mixed up and that "You lookin at me?" is from Taxi Driver, but Mum doesn't care. We get our make-up on and then we're rolling to a Fever soundtrack all the way to the Palace.

I've never been in the Palace before but something there makes you feel like you're part of a Hollywood Oscars Night – it's got lush red carpet everywhere, gold statues, fancy staircases, chandeliers and opera style balconies. Everything looks like it was commissioned by royalty. The ushers are in Penguin waistcoats and treat you like a million dollars ('Can I take Madam's coat?') People come in their best frocks as well as wild party costumes. We allow our coats to be whisked off to the cloakroom, then head to the Ladies for a quick mirror check. Mum does her 'You lookin at me?' line into the mirror again and two women in lipstick red bolero dresses start laughing at her. Then all three do a double-take. 'Is that Zowie?' one of the bolero women gasps.

'Baby doll?' Mum replies. 'Ooh baby baby... Marlene?'

They all squeal with excitement and start jumping about. It's one of Mum's old friends from when she had her flower shop. Before you know it, they're in the foyer doing selfies, Mum sandwiched between the three boleros, posing to the max. Mum squeezes me into the photos.

The PA system announces the show will start in five minutes. We rush to our seats. I've just enough time to text Marcus.

At Musical w Mum. Bit bored. But mum lovin evry mo. Watcha doin

He replies with

Homework

The music starts. We've got front row seats so we can see the sweat bubbling under the pancake make-up of Tony Moreno. He has film star looks, a growly hero voice and when he stands at the front of the stage, he speaks like he's addressing us the audience as much as the other members of the cast, which is fun. I look along my row. Eighteen females and one male. There are a few excited screams from the ladies when Tony Moreno does a hip wiggle, which makes others giggle and still others start shushing everybody. Then the mayhem starts. The first hit song comes on.

Instantly half the audience, including Mum, are on their feet. They flood into the aisles. A forearm rolling, fringe tickling, crotch jerking, finger-waving madness breaks out. The actors love it and do a synchronised dance along the edge of the stage with the audience in the aisle only two metres away. The whole building vibrates: the balconies, the ceiling with its roses and plaster babies and carefully draped Virgins in chariots, everything shakes to the music. As I'm dancing, I look up and notice a crack in the plaster ceiling appears to be getting wider. I look back down, thinking it's a trick of the lights. The floor is bouncing to the stomp of the ladies. Me and Mum swag it out. Everybody's singing at the top of their voices. Then Tony Moreno announces, 'It's night. It's fever. It's Night Fever!' I get my phone out and record Mum in the mayhem, then send it to Marcus.

Beats homework?

Lol is all he manages to reply. I file it under useless boyfriend.

In the interval Mum manages to arrange a seat swap so in the second half we join the Bolero Girls a few rows back and get our funk on, big style. I'm glad no one from school is here as the moves are so uncool, even though I love doing them.

At the bar afterwards, Mum gets lemonades. She hands me one and I swap mine with hers to check Mum's has no added vodka. Her friends are telling her their life stories. They've not met in fifteen years and they invite Mum to their Disco Revival exercise group and tell her they do singing and dancing for old folk's homes and cabarets for charity. Mum's amazed and everyone swaps phone numbers. Then Tony Moreno appears at the bar. There's a scream, followed by a mad scramble. Mum wants a signature and a kiss but she's also checking her watch. It's nearly midnight.

'Mum, you're not Cinderella,' I tell her, 'Your car won't turn into a pumpkin when the clock strikes twelve.'

'But what about school?'

'Duh. It's half term, remember?'

'But Anthony's alone!'

'He'll live. Unfortunately.'

Mum still dithers.

'Mum,' I say, 'you're allowed to have fun. Go to Mr Moreno.'

She kisses me then dives into the melee. I check my phone.

Tune! from Marcus. I think he's being sarcastic. I text him back.

Mum had a good time, that's what matters.

Tru. Wen I c u agen?

He didn't add even one kiss to the end of his last message so I don't reply.

200

Mum returns all flushed in a bit of a stampede of others. She's waving her signed Fever programme. 'He kissed me,' she says. 'Tony Moreno kissed me!'

'Amazing, Mum.'

'Then he did some moves with me and everyone cheered. Oh and a piece of plaster fell off the ceiling and everyone has to leave. We brought the house down! Me and Tony Moreno have brought the house down! Come on, we have to go.'

We drive home to her now personal friend, Tony Moreno's Fever sound track. Even when she's wandering in and out of her bedroom, she's still doing the moves, singing and la-la- la-ing where she can't remember the words. When I check on her again, she's snoring, face up on the bed in a frozen star jump. She's still dressed in her Tony Moreno outfit.

CHAPTER 27

A MAN CALLED GERALD

It's been ages and I've got credit, so next morning I phone Mikaela. It rings and rings and rings but eventually she picks up.

'How's you?'

'I'm good,' Mikaela replies.

'Why didn't you play the match?'

'Wasn't in the mood.'

'Fam?'

'I thought if I left the house, I'd be returning to a crime scene.'

'That bad?'

'It's World War One. Except I'm the one trapped in no-man's land.'

'But they're in the house together?'

'Dad spends all day under his car, Mum out in the garden cutting dead flowers off bushes. They don't speak. Mum asked me what I think about moving out with her. I don't want to move out. Where to?'

I'm listening for a sigh, but nothing comes.

'That's bad, Mikay.'

'At least I got double pocket money this week because Mum didn't ask Dad if I've been given any already. Kerching!'

She does this cold laugh down the phone.

'Your dad back yet?' she asks me.

'He's phoned a couple of times, talking to Mum. And they're not yelling. I think he expects Mum to wilt but she's holding up OK. I just don't want her to go back to drugging.'

'Not every dancing cow brings you milk.'

'Mikay?'

'It means beautiful things can be dangerous.'

I still don't understand her. I hear her mum shouting at her: "Come off the phone, Mikaela, you've been on it all day!"

'I've got to go, Dell,' she says.

'We have to meet up this half term.'

'Course.'

'Soon though.'

'OK ... Laters.'

'Gators.'

I've never heard Mikaela sound sadder. I can just see her staring out of her window twisting up her hair as her mum snaps away at bushes with a pair of giant scissors and her dad yanks at big lumps of metal under his car. It has to be bad because Mikaela's never missed a match before.

I spend the rest of the day practising football in the garden, trying not to think about Mikaela. In the evening, Mum starts hesitating about going to Disco Revival. She thinks maybe her old friends were just being nice to her and they don't really want her there.

'Go, Mum, you'll enjoy it. You get to wear your platforms and dance like you're saving the world from a giant octopus invasion.' I mime Mum's octopus-duel dancing.

Mum laughs. 'You sure?'

'Yes. It's a command. Go!'

Ten minutes later she spins out in full Moreno outfit, fighting octopuses.

I text Marcus.

What u doin

The Shuffle

Huh?

Will vid u

There's a minute wait, then a video starts buffering on my phone.

It's of Marcus. He's cutting up a rug in his living room, doing dance moves. He's good until his phone falls off something at the end. I text him back.

Not bad but watch

I balance my phone on my bedroom dresser and press record. Then bust some moves. I send it him:

Am way betta dan u

I wait. Another video starts buffering.

We spend the night battling dance moves.

Marcus signs off with:

I win. c ya gorgeous xx

I send him a spinning trophy and two kisses. Then I lie in my bed and wait for Mum to return. It gets past 11 pm. I thought Disco Revival finished at 9pm? At ten past midnight I finally hear her car drawing up. I get to the door just as Mum's opening it. Mum's drunk. I can see it instantly in her eyes. And there's a man who's not my dad on her arm.

'Who's he?' I ask, not letting him past.

Mum turns to look at him like it's the first time she's noticed him. 'Yes, who are you?' she says.

'My name's Gerald,' the man replies. I can see he likes mum and is concerned for her.

'Well, off you go then, Gerald!'

'Mum!'

The man hands me Mum's car keys, nods courteously to me and even more politely to Mum, then leaves.

Mum collapses on the sofa and laughs her face off.

MTB puts his head in the room. I can tell he's checking Mum's OK but he does a "not bothered" sneer, heads past us into the kitchen then walks out again, feeling his puny biceps with one hand and clutching a protein shake with the other. Mum gets herself upright on the sofa and reruns her arrival doing all the voices.

'Who's he?'

'Yes, who are you?'

'My name's Gerald.'

'I didn't know there were men at Disco Revival,' I tell her.

'Neither did I!' says Mum and she starts laughing again. I join in, I can't help it, it's the way mum says it.

'Those tablets, they're not working are they?' I ask her, when we've both got our straight faces on again.

'No, they ... I forgot to take them,' she says. 'Remind me next time.' She kisses me, then tries to get up from the sofa but has to sit down again. 'I have a headache,' she groans, 'and this back tooth's killing me, Adele. I need the tooth fairy.' She falls asleep on the sofa arm with her hands pressed to one side of her jaw. I can't move her.

I text Marcus.

If u eva wanna swap mums lemme no

Why

She drunk agen

Sorry x

Sok. Least she had fun x

CHAPTER 28

THE CONTRACT

Half term's over and we're in Form Class when Miss Fridge walks in. She nods to the form teacher then marches to the back of the class where me and Mikaela are. Mikaela's in one corner, I'm in another because we've been sat as far away from each other as possible as a punishment. Miss Fridge hesitates a moment, then comes up to me and whacks a piece of paper on my desk. It's a written-out contract. I read it:

I agree that I

☺ WILL NOT FIGHT ON THE FOOTBALL PITCH

☺ WILL NOT GET SENT OFF BY USING RUDE WORDS

☺ WILL PASS TO EACH OTHER PROPERLY

☺ WILL NOT ATTACK THE REFEREE, SPECTATORS OR OTHER PLAYERS

☺ WILL NOT LEAVE THE PITCH WHILE THE GAME IS ON

☺ WILL LISTEN TO THE COACH AND FOLLOW HER INSTRUCTIONS

She says we both have to sign it, else neither of us is playing in the Final this Saturday. I sign it. I want to play. Miss Fridge crosses the room to Mikaela. She slaps the paper down and stares at her. It's slightly amusing as Miss Fridge doesn't know that we're actually friends again, she thinks we're still enemies. Mikaela signs it.

'This is a binding contract. There'll be consequences if either of you break it!' Miss Fridge glowers, waving the paper in the air. She turns and walks stiff-legged out of the classroom.

Later in the playground, I go up to Mikaela, thinking it's good that we're friends, but as I approach she rolls her eyes, then starts pointing at me in little stabs. *One more time*, I think.

'What is the matter with you, Mikaela?'

'The whole world can know, I don't care. My mum's sleeping with that whore you call your dad now. Slut. Runs in the family I bet!'

Everyone's screaming "fight!" Mikaela grabs my blouse so I throw her down. We roll on the floor for a bit. I'm hitting her in the ribs, but she hardly fights back. I let go to see what she does. She puts her arms around me and squeezes my ribs, crying into my chest. I ask her what's the matter and she says her mum has moved out now, and she's only got her dad. 'It's a mess, Adele,' she says. 'It's all fucked up.'

I rest my arm on her back. 'Yeh, they fuck us up, our mums and dads.'

There's a crowd around us, gawping. 'What the fuck are yous looking at?' I shout. They slink away.

I think me and Mikaela are friends again. We walk back to class together, arm in arm. Everything is so confusing. I'm thinking, *is my dad really living with her mum now?*

CHAPTER 29

THE DREAM

It's morning. I text Marcus.

U deh

Yup

Can I fone u

Sure

I phone him.

'What's up?'

'I had this dream last night, I was going to the corner shop and I had to cross a patch of forest to get there and all these bodies were sleeping rough under blankets under the trees. They turned and looked right at me and every face was the same, a girl with a tear tattooed below her eye. In the trees above each one of her was a pair of football boots, dangling.'

'Did you recognise her?'

'No. She just stared and stared. Her face was a moon. There was a smashed bottle in the grass on the ground in front of me. I was in bare feet, running like a wolf, treading really carefully. My foot was right over the bottle.'

'And?'

'As my foot goes down, instead of getting cut, the ground underneath me disappears and it's like I've stepped off a cliff, I'm falling through the air. I'm screaming, petrified. Then I woke up.'

'Oh.'

It's weird on the phone, I can't see Marcus's face. I don't know what he's feeling.

'What does it mean then, the dream?' I ask him.

He makes some thinking noises on the phone, sucking his teeth, blowing air through his lips.

'Well?'

'Nothing' he says. 'Some dreams are just a big pile of nonsense. Come round. I haven't seen you in ages.'

Thinking Marcus would be useless as a clairvoyant, I pull on some jeans and a top and get a taxi to meet him on the bit of tarmac in the park near his house. When I get there, he's waiting for me.

'You OK?'

He takes my hand in his. His favourite football is under his arm. I feel better seeing him, it makes the dream seem, like he says, nonsense. We kick the ball around a bit then I sit on the low wall that surrounds the tarmac and he practices tricks. Afterwards, he comes up and stands in front of me, nudges his hips between my knees so he can get close and places his arms around me. I rest my head on the top of his head and gaze out across the park. A dog has stopped on the tarmac in front of us. It looks up at me, puzzled.

211

CHAPTER 30

THIN ICE

During one of her sigh sessions with me, Mum said she used to be a champion ice skater. So I hold her to it. She wriggles and squirms but it's no use and this Saturday afternoon we set off for the ice rink. Mum's nervous ("after all these years" etc). I haven't told her, but I've recruited some help to get her around.

Me and Mum get to the rink, check in our shoes and start loosening the laces on the skating boots we've hired. Mum keeps looking around. 'It's much smaller than I imagined,' she says.

'What age were you when you were a champion skater, Mum?'

'About eight,' Mum goes, then, 'when I say champion skater what I meant was I got a Certificate for getting round without falling over.'

I groan. I know now she's going to be as bad as me, if not worse. Luckily, my helper shows up. Mikaela. I'm thinking we can be on each side of my mum to push her round and help her up when she falls.

'Is this who I think it is?' says Mum as Mikaela comes up to us.

212

'It's Mikaela.'

'Whose mother is...'

'It's not Mikaela's fault, it's you adults who messed things up. She's my friend. Now don't kick off, Mum.'

I run up and grab Mikaela before Mum can give her the evil eye and turn her away. We high five. I take her hand and pull her with me to close the gap with my mum.

Mikaela shakes Mum's hand politely. I know Mikaela's been banned from seeing me in case we go shoplifting, so this is a big deal for her.

There's an awkward silence.

'Well, girls, let's get these boots on and skate,' says Mum.

The ice rink is a large circle of ice with benches around it going up about five rows. There's a cafe pumping out greasy fumes and cheesy tunes and polystyrene cups, there's a shop selling tat, there's stinking toilets and there's a PA system that blares – 'please can all skaters circulate in an anti-clockwise direction' every ten seconds, an instruction which none of the about hundred skaters or so – most of them kids who wouldn't know anti-clockwise from a slap in the face – pay any attention to.

'It's freezing,' I say.

'It *is* an ice rink,' Mikaela replies.

I give her my unimpressed look.

'Just sayin.'

Me and Mikaela tie each other's laces. We're all strapped up and ready. Mum is on the phone for a bit, but finally gets off it. Mikaela volunteers to go first. She clutches her way along the side-boards to the rink entrance, puts a foot though the opening and onto the ice, then another foot.

All her weight is on her arms which are clinging to the skirt boards. She gets herself upright, shifting her weight to her feet, gets herself steady, pushes off a tiny amount and promptly falls onto her bum. 'Yaaah!' she shouts. She scrambles up, chopping ice with her boots as she does, and clings to the skirt boards. She waves me to get on the ice too.

I get one foot on the ice and wobble a bit, get the other foot down and push myself off. I stay low with my feet wide to balance and my bum out to make sure I don't shoot forward too fast. I get a metre along the ice like this then someone zooming along at sixty miles an hour knocks into me and I fall down in a scream. Mikaela staggers over to me, reaches out a hand and tries to haul me up but the ice is too slippery and she only falls on top of me instead. Even Mum laughs.

'Your turn!' we call to Mum from our heap on the ice.

Mum crosses herself, then steps onto the ice.

And glides.

And glides.

And glides.

'Oh my God,' I say to Mikaela, 'my mum's like a swan!'

Mikaela gawps. 'That's your mum. Wowser. She can skate!'

We hold onto the boards and try to keep my mum in sight. She's bobbing and weaving between slower people, her hands behind her back, her body bent forward, her face all happy.

'Aagh!' I scream. She does a sudden twist and now she's actually skating backwards and waving at us at the same time.

'For real?' asks Mikaela, getting her phone out and taking a pic. We look but there's nothing but a blur. Mum's too fast even for Mikaela's phone.

After a bit more showboating, Mum pulls up alongside us.

'Mum! Mum! Mum! You have to teach us!'

'I don't know. I mean, I just skate. It all just came back.'

As Mum talks, me and Mikaela latch onto an arm of her each and, slipping and sliding, we get her to haul us around the rink. We move across the ice like a six-legged, three-headed centipede. Everyone overtakes us – tiny tots, old couples and smooth skaters, but we don't care.

We're all bundled together in a big ice ball after yet another tumble when suddenly Mikaela fishes out her phone and stares at it, worried. 'I've got to go,' she says.

'But we're having so much fun,' I protest.

'You sure?' my mum asks, disappointed.

'I liked ice skating with you, Mrs Vialli, but I need to get back.'

I can see the panic in Mikaela's eyes. I help her take off her skates on the benches. 'My dad's come back early and wants to know where I am,' Mikaela says. 'I just hope I switched off my phone's location thingy fast enough. I told him I was in the library.'

We hug and she runs off.

'What spooked her?' Mum asks.

'She thinks she left the bath running,' I lie.

Mum looks at me. She knows I've lied but she lets it slide. 'Come on, then,' she says, instead, 'Lesson one. How to push off.'

Mum shows me how to glide on one foot then switch to the other, and how you are meant to extend the amount of time between switching feet as you get better at it. With all my football skills, it doesn't take me too long to pick up the basic technique – after five falls I can actually glide twenty metres without ending on my bum.

The ice rink loudspeaker announces the rink is closing in ten minutes. We scoff some fish and chips from the cafe then jump in the car. As Mum pulls out of the ice rink car park, I text Marcus:

Can u skate

Wot u mean

Bin ice skatin w mum. Hopeless (me) can u

Im the best. Tho i neva tried it yet lol

Lol x

X

A Note From Mum

Thank you, Adele, you are a wonderful daughter. I love you very much xxx

Mum's started leaving these random notes. They make me feel good but I'm not sure what to make of them. I check with MTB and he says he's getting the notes as well. We decide Mum is doing some kind of therapy.

CHAPTER 31

FINAL PRACTICE

The Final is coming up fast and this is our last Practice session. We're one player short of a team which Miss Fridge says is perfect for sharpening us up by playing five a side. She has us doing zonal defence, pass and move, and long shooting.

After a liquids break, we do weaving through cones, jumping headers and tackling. We work hard. By the end, we're all dripping wet and dropping. Miss Fridge gees us up for five more minutes of long passing then relents. She calls us to sit round her so we can discuss tactics for the Final. The weather forecast is sopping wet so she wants long studs, tight marking and long range shooting. As she's explaining, Mikaela calls out.

'What's that scar, Miss?'

Miss Fridge is wearing shorts and there's a long, old scar running all the way up her left thigh into her shorts.

'I was knocked off my bike by a car. Didn't see me. Broke my leg, my hips. They told me "Julie, you'll never walk again."'

'That's your name, Miss – Julie?' Mikaela says.

'Yes.'

'Did it hurt?' asks someone else.

'It hurt a lot. Not the pain, though that was hard. I was a champion footballer and that car ended my dream.'

'But you move OK, Miss. You don't limp or anything.'

'I can't run though for more than ten seconds, then my hips hurt like hell. And I can't have children. So you're my children. And you're my football.'

'You were good?'

'Yes.'

'Show us your skills!' everyone shouts.

Miss takes up the challenge. 'Give me the ball, girls!'

Someone rolls her the ball. Miss flicks it up, catching it in the crook of her neck. She lets it drop to the crook of her knee then flicks it back up again, high. While it's in the air, she drops to the ground and sits down. Then, when the ball drops, she immediately ping pongs it between her left and right feet. She does scissors switches. Then she rolls onto her front and keeps the ball up with the flat of her trainers. I've never seen anyone do that last trick before. She's better even than Marcus.

Everyone starts clapping.

Miss catches the ball in her hands. 'That's it girls, my hips can't take any more. Do your best tomorrow. Do me proud.'

Miss lets us take an extra-long blast in the showers. We all walk off the school grounds, buzzing. Then me and Mikaela are at the bus stop together.

'"Julie"? I always had her down as a Susannah or something,' Mikaela says.

'Me too!'

I catch Mikaela sighing. 'How's it going at home?' I ask.

'Dad's put a lock on their bedroom door.'

'What! He's locked your mum in?'

'No, out. Of their bedroom.'

'So your mum's back?'

Mikaela nods. 'But it's ridiculous now. One tells me something like, "ask your mother where's the oven glove?" then I have to ask my mum, and take the answer back.'

'At least they're together.'

'If that's what you call it.'

I squeeze her hand. 'Stay strong.' I say. It's what she always says to me.

She sniffs. 'How's your boyfriend?'

'Marcus is OK.'

'It's not fair. You've got a boyfriend and a brother, I've got nobody!'

'You've got me.'

Suddenly Mikaela's squeezing me like she's never going to let go.

When her bus comes, she gets on it and I wave to her. She hardly waves back, she's so preoccupied.

Later, she texts me.

hws yr mum?

OK

Yr dad shwd up?

no

Sry

sok. nt yr folt

my parents doin counslin. i think theyl split agen. stil gna get dat mnth in Jmca tho. They owe me ☺

Ded rite.

CHAPTER 32

THE CUP FINAL

It's morning and it's the Final. Mum's had to go for an emergency dental appointment and can't watch. Dad's nowhere. There's only one touchline that is not under a foot of water and that's where all the spectators are gathered. Suddenly I spot MTB. I have to look again. He waves. There's a bunch of classmates next to him in various disastrous outfits. (e.g. Winona in pink Hello Kitty ear muffs, red leggings and yellow jockey boots). Then parents and more parents. Among them I pick out Mikaela's mum and dad, stood together stiffly under an umbrella as black as the clouds.

I weigh the opposition up. Worthington Academy are tall, focused athletes. We have titchy Report Card recruits in defence and a couple of Detention Room conscripts in midfield. It's not looking good.

Worthington kick off. They boot the ball high up in the air then charge after it like a herd of stampeding buffalo. Our conscripts take fright. Me, Mikaela and a few others try to hold them up, flinging ourselves this way and that, but it's useless. Mikaela throws herself onto the goal line twice to stop goals and gets coated in mud and line markings, but in the end we can't keep the ball out. Worthington are soon hammering us.

At half time, Miss Fridge is furious. 'What is wrong with you lot? You should be ashamed of yourselves!' She flings her clipboard into the mud and stomps off to lean against a grass rolling machine with her head in her hands. I think she's crying. We all look at each other, wondering what happens now.

MTB's hovering. I edge over to him. 'What should we do?'

My brother shrugs. 'Don't give up. Anything can happen.'

Miss walks back over to us and waves for us to come close. We gather round her again. 'Go out there and do your best, girls. Remember your positions, keep your heads. Pass. Move. Tackle. Do me proud. OK?'

The referee blows for the second half to start. The rain begins hammering down and the ball sticks in the mud like it's glued. Everyone's slipping and sliding. I manage to score from a direct free kick but there's no miraculous comeback and we lose 5–1. I trudge back to the changing rooms, dress, leave. My brother's waiting. For once he doesn't tease me. We get a taxi and ride in silence. He's never been to a match of mine before. This is the first time. I wish he'd seen me win.

I break the silence. 'Well?'

'You played good, Sis.'

'5–1?'

'You played good though.'

Coming from MTB, this is high praise.

Mum calls down to us when we get home. She's in bed.

'How did it go?' she asks when we enter her room. She's got her back to us. I can't see any bottles. The air smells OK.

'We lost,' I say flatly.

'But she was brilliant,' adds MTB, 'she chased every ball, never gave up.'

Mum turns round. 'She's my daughter, of course she's brilliant! Come here, darling.'

Mum gives me a hug. She's got a big swelling on her left cheek and she smells of dental disinfectant. It's nice hearing her praise me even if she wasn't there.

'Are you OK, Mum?' I ask.

Mum sighs. 'I need my phone, she says, 'and a ... a ...' She falls asleep.

CHAPTER 33

AN ENDING OF SORTS

I wish I could say everything turned out OK apart from the football. That me and Mikaela got on great like before. That my mum and dad got back together. That Mum never drank again and never danced bad disco moves again in front of my friends. But like I warned at the beginning, life sometimes doesn't work out like that.

The day after we lost the Final, my dad phoned me:

'Hi Adele, it's me.'

'Hi, Dad.'

'How's your mum?'

'Why don't you ring her and ask her yourself?'

'I'm only asking.'

'She's OK.'

'I'm sorry, Adele. For the whole mess.'

'You mean abandoning us?'

'I never abandoned you. I'm always here for you.'

'Where's that?'

'... On the end of the phone. I'm a bit between places at the moment.'

I wonder where between places is. Under a railway arch?

In a swanky hotel? In some other woman's bed?

'Mum's fine actually, she's having fun,' I say.

'I can see that from my credit card bill. Is there any shop she hasn't visited in Manchester?'

It's Dad's attempt at a joke.

'... I miss you, Adele.'

'You should have thought of that when you left us, Dad.'

Mum calls me. I put the phone down.

I'm sure many kids have had this same conversation and will be reading this saying, "been there, got the T shirt".

So this is the end. As a special treat since you reached it (The End! Yay!) below are two more school essays and a shortcut for French homework. Sorry I haven't done my Patriarchy essay yet, you'll have to wait for that one.

Martin Luther King and Civil Disobedience.

Martin Luther King was a great man. After Rosa Parks's bus protest he led marches everywhere and was arrested and jailed for equal rights including civil disobedience. He did long speeches. In my view, civil disobedience is a bit iffy. Sometimes you have to do more than stop buses from running and lying down in the streets. Sometimes you have to fight, not lie down. Martin Luther King was shot. Officially a lone gunman did it but I believe it was a government conspiracy because he was too dangerous to the social order.

Teacher's Comments:

4 out of 10.
Well done for your passionate arguments here, Adele. However, an essay must be longer than one paragraph and you go off the subject with your final sentence. Please show me your mind map before you write your next essay.

How To Make Apple Crumble

You need sugar, flour, cup of water, apples (like, obviously!). Mix everything except the apples together. Chop the apples up and put them in a baking dish. Then add the mixed up goop. Put it all in the oven on high and wait 30 minutes, watching it does not burn.

Alternatively you could get a life and buy one from the local supermarket.

Teacher's Comments:

Did you compare the home-made one with the shop bought one? Which tasted better? The proof of the pudding is in the eating. Adele!

French Homework: Learn 10 New Words

Le keeper – keeper
Le football – football
Le weekend – weekend
Le but – goal
Un come-back glorieux – glorious comeback
Jouer au foot – play football
La Coupe du monde – World Cup
Le ballon – the ball
Le meilleur buteur – top goal scorer
Le fin – the end

DON'T MISS
THE OTHER BOOKS
IN THE STRIKER SERIES

'I enjoyed reading the book from the beginning to the end. YA fiction for all ages'
Assia Shahin – blogger - http://assiashahin.blogspot.it

'An amazing book and it would benefit people, whether they are hard of hearing or not.
Robert Murrell, age 13, profoundly deaf and wears hearing aids.
(Reviewed for the National Deaf Children Society)

'Full to the brim with the joy, heartache and passion for the beautiful game.'
Carnegie Medal winner Melvin Burgess

'A strong inspirational story about human aspiration.'
Commonwealth Writers' Prize shortlisted Jacob Ross

'Touching, funny and well tackled!'
Muli Amaye, novelist

'A story that takes you through every emotion a young schoolboy goes through.'
Dotun Adebayo, BBC Radio 5

'An excellent book! This read quite a lot like a Jacqueline Wilson book with Pakistani characters.'
Ms Yingling Reads, Teacher / Librarian/Blogger, USA

'Mehmood gives us a sterotype-quashing, timely novel about religion, gender, and families.   You're Not Proper sounds a resonant, authentic note that cuts through the monotone voices coming out of YA writing'
Dr Claire Chambers, Huffington Post

'You're Not Proper is a real insight into communities more often talked about than listened to.
Full of heart and a cracking good read as well. Highly recommended!'
Melvin Burgess

'Contemporary and hard-hitting. High on impact and highly engaging' **Jake Hope**, *critic, librarian and coordinator of the Lancashire Children's Book of the Year Award.*

Lightning Source UK Ltd.
Milton Keynes UK
UKOW04f1148280815

257694UK00002B/16/P